GUNS AT CHINOOGA PEAK

Doug Machin's world collapsed on account of returning a favour. He had called on Dave Caswall of the Flying Diamond, offering to take a thousand head of beef on his drive to St Louis. When Sam Caswall returned from town with stores, Dave Caswall was dead, and Sheriff Jake Caswall of Springfield made no delay in setting bounty hunter Moss Hanney the chore of bringing in Doug, dead or alive! Fate threw another pair of dice. Marshal Travis and his Deputy arrived in Springfield with time to kill. They stirred up intrigue, suspense and violent action in the final act at Chinooga Peak.

GUNS AT CHINOOGA PEAK

GUNS AT CHINOOGA PEAK

by

Hal Jons

The Golden West Large Print Books
Long Preston, North Yorkshire,
BD23 4ND, England.

British Library Cataloguing in Publication Data.

Jons, Hal
        Guns at Chinooga Peak.

        A catalogue record of this book is
        available from the British Library

        ISBN   978-1-84262-891-1 pbk

First published in Great Britain in 1983 by Robert Hale Ltd.

Cover illustration © Michael Thomas

The moral right of the author has been asserted

Published in Large Print 2014 by arrangement with
Hal Jons, care of Mrs M. Kneller

The Golden West Large Print is an imprint of Library Magna
Books Ltd.

Printed and bound in Great Britain by
T.J. (International) Ltd., Cornwall, PL28 8RW

ONE

Sheriff Caswall glanced up as the shadows blocked out the sunlight from the street, and his handsome face carried a scowl as he took his hand away from the bottle that stood in the open drawer.

Two men stepped into the office and the light shone through again, allowing him to study them. He cursed inwardly as he saw the marshal's badge on the smaller of the two men, a mere six-footer; the other man, also toting a badge, was a gangling youngster, with hands like hams and a sloppy grin on his face.

'Yeah! What can I do for you?' Caswall asked in a flat voice, totally devoid of interest.

The marshal pulled a chair out and took his time getting settled, then he pushed the other chair out for his companion before addressing the sheriff. 'I'm US Marshal Travis and my pardner's US Deputy Marshal Wallace, and I reckon, if that shingle over the door's up to date, you're Jake Caswall, Sheriff of Springfield County?'

The sheriff nodded. 'The shingle don't lie none.' He eased back in his chair and waited for his visitors to state their business, surveying them out of cold, deep-brown eyes.

Travis looked bland, but he was weighing up the sheriff carefully as he spoke. 'I'd like to know what Moss Hanney is doing in your town. Marshal Wallace saw him leaving this office before calling at Oakham's store. He was laying in stores when I left.'

Temper showed in Caswall's eyes, and his reply was quick. 'If you're so all-fired curious, why in heck didn't you ask him.'

Travis leaned forward slightly, and his expression was cold. The vacuity had left Wallace's face, and his blue eyes were watchful.

'I'm asking you again, Sheriff Caswall, and this time I want to know.'

Caswall didn't answer immediately, but he opened another drawer and shuffled through some papers, then pulled one out and passed it across the table. 'That'll explain what Hanney's doing here. Anyway, it's my business; I like to handle things my own way in Springfield and I've got no call to ask yore office for help.'

Carl Travis read the missive, which was dated three days earlier, and initialled and sent by the telegraphist of the Butterfield stage office. It was addressed to M. Hanney, Arkansas Hotel, Las Animas, and read '1,000 dollars and reasonable expenses for capture dead or alive of Doug Machin, the killer of Dave Caswall, owner of Flying Diamond, Springfield County.' Travis passed the paper along the table to Joe Wallace, who digested the contents and returned his attention to the scowling sheriff.

'How come you're sitting on your fan, instead of heading a posse chasing the killer?' Travis asked quietly.

'I don't have to answer that question, mister,' Caswall growled. 'But I'll tell you. Dave Caswall was my father, so I guess if I was chasing Doug Machin, the killer, there's only one way he'd come back to Springfield, an' that's draped over his bronc. Another thing, my brother Clem is mighty close to Machin's sister, so any more blood-letting in the family wouldn't do them much good. It'd be too much to live down.'

Travis considered a little, then nodded. 'Yeah, I guess that sounds reasonable to me. The trouble is that Moss Hanney's got a reputation for claiming on dead men only. Now I'll allow that's mighty fine for Hanney, but he's gotten rich denying a lot of men a fair trial.'

Sheriff Caswall snorted. 'A trial wouldn't help Machin any. He'd as likely be lynched if he was brought for trial in Springfield. My pa was mighty popular in this neck of the woods.'

Carl Travis stood up and pushed his chair back under the table, and Joe Wallace followed suit; then nodding curtly to Sheriff

Caswall they stepped through the door back into the sunlight. Caswall grunted his displeasure at their interruption before reaching for the bottle of rye that was his constant balm.

On the sidewalk Travis leaned over the rail, with the Panhandle saloon behind him, and surveyed the length of Main Street. Joe Wallace eased alongside him and watched the Butterfield coach enter town from the north in a swirl of dust, to come to rest in front of the staging-office. Both lawmen watched the stocky, bewhiskered driver climb down and open the door before clambering to the roof, ready to hand down suitcases. Eight women stepped out of the coach and were directed to the Gold Rush saloon opposite the depot, and from nowhere eager men gathered round to carry their suitcases. Then the twittering, excited females squealed their delighted way across the street, totally engulfed by their admiring escorts.

The dust settled and the batwing doors stopped swinging, then Travis turned to Wallace. 'Any thoughts, Joe?' he asked.

Joe Wallace passed a massive hand over his face and concentrated his mind on what had transpired in Sheriff Caswall's office. 'The first thing that strikes me is that young Machin's due for his come-uppance whether or no he killed Dave Caswall. The other thing is that Machin is fairly handy with the

10

hardware, or Sheriff Caswall would have tailed him, no matter what he says 'bout not querying his brother's pitch with Machin's sister. In my book that sheriff don't think of anyone's feelings but his own.'

Carl Travis smiled and nodded as he searched his pockets for a cheroot. His protégé was coming along well, relying on his instincts.

'Yeah, I go along with what you say, Joe. Still, as Caswall said, it's none of our business. Moss Hanney is a registered bounty hunter, so having signed him up for the chore of bringing in Machin, Caswall's done all that he needs to do.'

''Cept for one thing,' Joe remarked slowly. 'Hanney was signed up to bring in Machin dead or alive, an' that tells me Caswall wants him dead very much, and quick. And when anybody wants to cut out a trial you can bet there's a durned good reason for it. I guess if we wanted to make sure Machin gets that trial we could make it our business.'

'Well, we've got ten days spare before we head for Santa Fe,' replied Travis. 'We can either spend it eating our heads off an' getting soft lying in a bed every night, or taking a look at things here in Springfield. It's up to you, this being your first holiday.'

Wallace grinned – Travis knew only too well that he could eat for the entire ten days quite cheerfully – but his answer came readily

11

enough. 'Let's give things the once-over before we move on.'

'Right.' Carl eased himself away from the rail as he spoke. 'This one's up to you, Joe. I'll follow your lead. Let's get ourselves a beer while you do some thinking.'

Joe followed his boss through the batwing doors of the Panhandle, his mind whirling a bit at having the responsibility for the case handed to him; but by the time he set the beers on their table he had regained control of his thoughts. He knew there was no way that Travis would let him miss any pointers, so he relaxed with his drink.

They were halfway through their beer when Moss Hanney pushed through the batwing doors and stalked up to the counter. The barkeep saw him coming and moved with alacrity to take his order. Hanney bellied up to the bar, then turned round to run his eyes over every corner of the saloon. He included Travis and Wallace in the sweep, but his face gave nothing away.

The man looked as cold as a mortician, thin and cadaverous, with a sallow complexion and lank, dark hair lying limp over his forehead. He was dressed completely in black leather, an altogether macabre figure, and the piercing eyes, as bright as live coals, made him look the personification of evil. The Colts, tied low against his skinny thighs, had the shine of usage.

A shudder of revulsion ran through Joe Wallace as he considered the man's chosen trade, but he continued to watch the bounty-hunter as Hanney tossed down a couple of brimming glasses of rye, stuffed two bottles into the deep pockets of his ankle-length coat, and took his change from the barkeep before returning to the street.

'I reckon he primes himself up to the eyeballs with liquor before going in for the kill,' Wallace said sourly.

Travis shook his head. 'I doubt if he touches a drop of that gut-rot before he's got his quarry hogtied for the ride back. The way I've heard it, he enjoys his job and don't need help out of a bottle to get it done.'

The Marshal drained his glass and caught Joe's eye. 'Well, where do we go from here?'

'Outside, to keep an eye on Hanney in case he leaves town, and to ask about old man Caswall's murder, like where and when it happened, and where his ranch lies, and to pay a visit to Machin's spread to see his sister.'

Travis gave the youngster an appreciative grin. 'I guess that should take care of today.'

'Mebbe we should take a meal first,' Joe tried, tentatively, and Carl looked at him in wonder. Wallace had eaten enough for four ordinary men just an hour and a half ago.

'You go and get yourself a meal, Joe,' Travis answered, 'and I'll collect the cayuses an' mebbe ask a few questions.'

Joe Wallace grunted his pleasure and they stepped out together along the sidewalk until they came abreast of the eating-house. Travis continued to the end of Main Street, where the livery stables and paddocks were set back off the rough road that pointed north towards Lamar.

A youngish man with a decided limp emerged from the gloom of a box, holding a long-handled hayfork, and eyed Travis questioningly. 'Which of 'em is yours, Marshal?' he asked.

'That big, shaggy-coated crittur in the end box,' Carl answered, pointing to the furthest box on the right. 'I'll take the bay mustang in the next box at the same time. My pard's feeding his face, so I'll save him some time.'

The man moved up the cobbled divide just ahead of Travis, then stopped at the stall housing the red stallion. 'You've sure got a big ugly crittur there, Marshal. I've spent a bit of time looking at him, and I'd say he's chock-full of running and guts. He don't take too kindly to other folk handling him neither, which ain't bad. I like a cayuse to show his preference.'

Travis smiled as he walked past the man into the box and stroked the big nose as the stallion turned his head to nuzzle him. 'Yeah, I guess he's all you say,' he remarked. 'He's always done all I've asked of him.'

The livery-man went to the end wall and hung the fork from a couple of nails, then came back to the box. 'I'll saddle up the bay if you like,' he said.

'I'd be much obliged, mister,' Carl answered. 'And mebbe at the same time you can tell me anything you know about the killing of the rancher, Dave Caswall. Just so you know who's asking, my moniker's Travis.'

'You ain't got no call to be asking about that killing, Marshal!' The voice was harsh, metallic, laden with menace, and both the marshal and the livery-man swivelled to stare at Moss Hanney, who had soft-shoed his way in. 'That killing's my business. I've been hired by the law to bring the killer in, so you can forget about it. When I go after any hombre, I bring him in, that's for sure.'

Carl Travis eased the stallion aside and stepped out of the box to eye the bounty-hunter coolly. 'You know durned well, Hanney, that the law is my business wherever in the United States I might find myself. You might have carved yourself a reputation for hunting down killers, but you cut no ice with me. I'm telling you before you set out that unless you bring in Machin alive I'll see to it you don't get paid.'

Hanney's eyes seemed to spark fire as he glanced briefly at Travis. 'There's no way you can stop me getting paid, Travis. There's a dodger being sent around saying dead or alive, so if I've got to load Machin with lead to bring him in, I will.'

Travis shrugged, and re-entered the box to saddle up his mount, while Hanney dug into his pocket for some coins, which he tossed to the livery man before entering a stall near to the door to saddle up a coal-black Morgan gelding.

The marshal and livery-man took their time, and at length the bounty-hunter led the Morgan into the sunlight without another glance in their direction.

'He gives me the creeps,' the livery-man said. 'Anyway, I was going to say when he snuck in, my moniker's Luke Withers. My old man, Jed Withers, owns the livery, but I do most of the work these days.' He paused, considering what Travis had asked him earlier. 'There's not much I can tell you about the killing of Dave Caswall. It seems like Clem, Frank and Ike Holland, the top-hand, were just leaving old Dave and heading for the brush country with all hands, when Doug Machin arrived to see the old man. They passed the time of day with him as he tied his cayuse to the hitch-rail. It was Sam Caswall who found the old man dead when he got back with Daley and Smart from town with the wagon. They'd gone into town before sun-up.'

'Four brothers, eh?' mused Travis. 'How do they get along?'

'Mighty close,' Withers answered quickly. 'I guess they've been kingpins on this range for a long time, but the old man was the boss. He always held the purse strings. Mind, he never kept those hellion sons of his short; I guess he liked to see 'em roistering around, showing off the Flying Diamond.'

'Which of the brothers gives the orders?' Carl asked.

'Seeing 'em together you'd reckon they all had equal say, but I've seen Frank look at 'em straight an' give an order, an' nobody's argued. He's the oldest, an' for my money a durn sight more ornery than old Dave when he's riled.'

'How about the one who's sweet on the Machin girl ... er, Clem, that is?'

Luke Withers looked at Travis sharply, then answered readily. 'I guess Clem's got the good looks an' sweet-talk for all four of 'em, but I'd sooner cross the others than him.'

'Well, I'm mighty obliged,' Carl said, as he backed Red out of his stall. 'Er, that Doug Machin. What sort of hombre is he?'

Withers didn't answer until he had backed Wallace's mustang out of its stall to stand in front of Red. He came close to Travis and his look was direct. 'Doug Machin's been a friend of mine a long time, Marshal, an' I've been mighty glad of it. He got me back to enjoying life again when the accident to my

17

leg stopped me forking a cayuse, and if he gunned down old Dave Caswall then he had a durned good reason for it, but I don't think there's anything would have got Doug to do that in cold blood.'

Travis nodded his thanks and followed the livery-man who led Wallace's mustang outside into the sunshine.

'You coming back, Marshal?' Withers asked, and when Travis grunted assent he pointed to an iron pot standing against the building. 'You'll find a key in that if the place is locked up, and the same two stalls empty.'

Travis held on to the mustang's lead rein as he climbed astride Red; then with a friendly smile at Luke Withers, he rode back up Main Street to stop outside the eating-house and tie the animals to the hitch-rail before seeking out Wallace inside. Joe had a plate of plum duff in front of him and a happy expression on his face, so Carl got himself a coffee and primed the younger man with all he had divined from Withers, and about the meeting with Moss Hanney in the livery-stable.

Joe paused with the last huge spoonful of duff poised ready. 'That Hanney, do you reckon he's heading for the Machin spread?' When Carl nodded, he continued: 'I'd like to be there when he turns up. Maybe we can give Machin's sister some protection.'

18

It took all of three hours for Travis and Wallace to get within sight of the Lazy Y home graze. The trail was clear cut, but the trail blazers seemed to have favoured meandering to physical effort, for at no point did it take to the rounded hills. Just out of Springfield the Flying Diamond trail forked away to the left to breast a rugged-looking hill. Maybe it signified nothing; it could be on account that the Flying Diamond punchers were thirstier than those of the Lazy Y.

They reined in and quartered the terrain to the distant ranch-house building and corrals. There were bunches of cattle dotted around, and even at the distance both Travis and Wallace could make out a few men along the corral rails. A lone horseman was headed north.

'Well, Hanney didn't take the easy route,' Joe remarked, 'but I can't see a cayuse hitched in front of the house. He should have been there long ago.'

'Uh – that's not his style, Joe,' Travis replied. 'He'll have covered every inch of this territory before he calls at the Lazy Y. If young Machin is laying up close to home, then Hanney'll be reckoning on having worked out the likeliest places before asking questions.' Carl turned in the saddle and studied his young deputy. 'How're you gonna handle it, Joe?'

19

Wallace rubbed his chin reflectively. 'I don't rightly know,' he confessed. 'Depends how much savvy Machin's sister's got. Telling her Hanney's on her brother's trail might spook her off to take some action that'll pop him into Hanney's net.'

Travis' smile was enough to tell Joe he was on the right tack, so he eased his mount forward. 'C'mon then, let's go and get acquainted.' Travis nodded, and brought his horse alongside.

Fifteen minutes later they rode into the Lazy Y compound, and a few punchers stopped their horse-breaking to come to the corral rails, and the men at the rails detached themselves and came to meet the two lawmen, who pulled up and eyed them blandly.

'You hombres wanting something?' The speaker stood out front of the other two, a tall, well-knit man in his mid-twenties, appraising the lawmen out of calm, grey eyes.

'Yeah, we'd like a word with Miss Machin concerning her brother,' Travis replied quietly. 'You can tell her it's Marshal Travis and Deputy Marshal Wallace called to see her.'

'Well, my moniker's Hank Ormond, ramrod of this outfit,' the man snapped, 'and if she don't want to talk to you there's no way you will!'

'You know better than that, Ormond,'

Travis said without rancour. 'We've got a job to do, and nothing stops us from doing it.'

'I guess your job is tracking down Doug. That, I can't deny, is yore right, but you've got no call to try using his sister to help you.'

'Now look, Ormond!' Joe Wallace put in. 'We're not blaming you protecting the young woman; it's just that it may be better she spoke to us before the bounty-hunter, Moss Hanney, shows up. He set out from Springfield ahead of us. I guess he's sizing up the territory before paying a visit.'

Ormond's face clouded over. Moss Hanney's name set him worrying. 'Those doggone Caswalls!' he snarled. 'They want Doug dead! No trial! Just Hanney, to make the execution legal.'

'Yeah. That's so,' Travis said. 'Jake Caswall sent to Las Animas for Hanney, offering $1,000 for Doug Machin, dead or alive. Now, we don't know one way or another whether Machin killed Dave Caswall, but we don't believe in dispensing with trials, and we do like to prove without doubt a man is guilty before he pays the penalty. So it may be by talking to us Miss Machin will best help her brother. If she wants you there when we palaver we've got on objection.'

Ormond nodded, satisfied. 'I'll go and see.' Then turning to his companions. 'See to their cayuses; give 'em a good feed an' a brush-down.' Then, as the lawmen slid out of their saddles, he hurried towards the ranch-house.

TWO

Moss Hanney removed the spy-glass from his eye with a grunt of annoyance. The glass had brought the little knot of men in front of the Machin ranch-house seemingly close enough to touch, and he'd had no difficulty in recognizing Marshal Travis and his deputy. He cursed long and fluently; Hanney was used to a clear field and he couldn't understand why the two lawmen wanted to horn in. There was no reward at the end of the trial for them, and nobody could have sent for them in the time that had elapsed since the killing. He bottled up his bad humour and reached for a cheroot, then sat back on his haunches to smoke it. He considered Travis as he sucked at the weed, and concluded that the man wouldn't be shaken from his course easily. Some lawmen had the crazy notion that a killer automatically deserved a trial, and would go to extraordinary lengths to see they got one; he guessed that Travis would insist upon it more than most.

Characteristically, he changed his mind. It had been his intention to visit the Machin girl after first lining up the territory, but now he decided he'd spend more time watching every movement out of the Lazy Y before making contact. If by some lucky chance he caught sight of Machin, then he would kill him, take a quick reward and dispel all argument, but he hoped the lawmen would find work elsewhere, leaving him the pleasure of flushing Machin into a long run, during which he, Hanney, could afford himself the pleasure of all sorts of villainy, blaming Machin on the way and keeping himself clear at the end of the road with some well-directed lead.

In his early days as a bounty-hunter he had merely earned his money, but with the years bitterness had permeated his being until his every thought was evil. He now took his pleasures where and as he could, and where his actions brought possibilities of retribution he removed victims with as little regard as he did the fugitives he followed with such deadly persistence. His crimes he reported as the handiwork of the man on the run. As always, there was no-one to argue the case for the corpse on the led-horse.

Taking up again his position of surveillance, Hanney quartered the terrain with the eyepiece, and concluded that the hills behind the Machin headquarters, being limestone, would most likely provide caves or holes where Machin could lie up and be kept topped up with provisions. He selected a likely fold on the opposite hill as a good place

24

to keep all movement under his eye; then, rejoining his mount, swung himself into the saddle and set off on a devious route to arrive at the selected spot.

The girl stepped away from the big, open fireplace, her anxious eyes fixed upon the two lawmen who followed Hank Ormond into the comfortable-looking room. She stopped beside a heavy, redwood table, and looked to Ormond for the introductions. Travis and Joe eyed her, and nodded a greeting, both momentarily spellbound by the girl's exquisite beauty. She wore shoulder-length, corn-gold hair, surrounding a smooth-skinned face of peach complexion, with eyes of cobalt blue and generous, well-shaped mouth. She was dressed for riding in a plain habit with divided skirt and knee-length boots.

'This is Marshal Travis, Miss Sally,' said Ormond; then, indicating Joe, 'and Deputy Marshal Wallace.'

'Howdy, Ma'am,' Carl and Joe said, almost in unison.

The girl made no immediate response, but motioned them to take seats at the table, and nodded when Ormond looked towards the side-table holding bottles and glasses.

Travis and Wallace took seats as the ramrod brought over bottles and glasses, and upon his invitation they poured slugs of Old

Crow while he poured a tiny drop for his boss and a mansize glass for himself from a bourbon bottle.

'Well. What is it that you want from me?' Sally Machin asked, after they had all sipped at their drinks. Her voice was low-pitched and husky, but the huskiness was caused by emotion that she had difficulty in keeping from showing.

'To put it bluntly, Miss, we want you to tell us anything you know of the whereabouts of your brother.' Carl Travis watched the girl intently as he spoke, and he saw the fight gleam out of the deep-blue eyes.

'If I knew where he was I wouldn't be telling you,' she answered firmly. 'My brother's no killer, Mister Travis, and I wouldn't set anybody on his trail. He had no call to kill Dave Caswall. He had called on him to offer a favour.'

'If your brother is innocent, Miss Machin, I guess we'll be setting out to prove it,' Joe Wallace put in, and as she glanced at him she saw compassion in his young face. 'Nobody gets rushed into a lynching party when we're around, an' nobody gets robbed of a fair trial. Mind, if it's proved that a man's guilty, then he'll pay the penalty.'

Sally Machin shook her head. 'That's all as maybe,' she said, 'but if he were guilty or not, I wouldn't point anyone in his direction if I knew.'

Hank Ormond was watching the two lawmen closely, judging how they were taking the girl's refusal to cooperate with them, and Travis could see the concern for the girl in the man's face. Ormond made to say something, then after another glance at the girl, stifled it back, and Travis guessed that the ramrod wanted the girl to make the first overtures. So he addressed the girl tersely: 'Yore brother's gonna need all the help he can get if he's innocent, and he's gonna need it mighty fast. The bounty-hunter, Moss Hanney, has been given the chore of bringing him in on a dead or alive basis, an' you can believe me that Hanney don't make problems for himself; he always brings 'em in dead. He's already on yore range makin' himself familiar with it.'

Sally Machin's hand went up to her throat, and her face paled visibly. She cast a quick look at Ormond, who looked back, unadulterated misery on his face. Then he squared his shoulders and gave the lawman a hard look. 'Well, Mister Travis, no-one's gonna deny Doug Machin a proper trial, an' if Hanney's on this range then he'll need watch his back, because no matter where young Doug is, I'll get Hanney before he gets Doug, an' that's for sure.'

'No Hank! No!' Sally Machin cried. 'There's no call for you to murder anyone on Doug's account. You know as well as I do

27

that he didn't kill Dave Caswall.'

'Hanney doesn't get to asking questions, Miss Sally,' Ormond replied bitterly. 'Once he gets his man in his sights he winds his business up. I've heard of him.'

Both Travis and Wallace kept silent while the ramrod and his boss stared back at each other, the man grim-faced, the girl caught up in indecision. After a long minute, the girl took hold of herself and she turned her attention to the lawman. 'If I knew where my brother was, and told you, how would that help him? The way I see it he'd still end up in gaol with a trumped-up charge over his head, and as likely to die on account of it as surely as if the bounty-hunter had got him first. Maybe when it comes down to cases, you're no better than Hanney.'

Both men shrugged the girl's last remark aside, and Joe Wallace leaned nearer to the girl to hold her attention. 'Tell us about the favour that your brother intended doing for Dave Caswall, which was the reason for his visit.'

The girl was surprised at the young lawman's change of direction, but answered readily enough. 'We're about ready to take a herd to St Louis for my uncle, Sam Machin; he's a buyer and shipper of St Louis. Doug called in on Dave Caswall that morning offering to take up to a thousand head of Flying Diamond beef. Both Doug and Hank reckoned that four thousand head isn't much more sweat than three thousand. Anyway, Uncle Sam can handle four thousand, and hold a steady price if we can get them to St Louis three months from now.'

'That's a mighty neighbourly offer, Miss Machin,' Joe replied. 'Have the Machins and Caswalls always been that friendly?'

'I guess so. Now and again some of the hands fall out and cause a bit of trouble, but there's no regular feuding, and there's never any stock trouble.'

'How come Sheriff Caswall sent for Hanney with a dead or alive option? There's nothing friendly in that,' Travis put in.

'Because he's a deadbeat!' Hank Ormond barked. 'He got himself voted into the sheriff's job to save himself forkin' a cayuse an' gettin' clogged with alkali chasin' dogies every which way. He likes to have a bottle within reach from sun-up to sun-down, an' there's no way he'd head a posse if he could farm the chore to anyone else. Makin' it a dead or alive order is just his way to dodge any responsibility for a trial.'

'How about the other brothers?' Travis asked. 'Any of them been looking for your brother, Miss?'

'Clem looked in the next day,' Sally replied, 'but he wasn't ready to pin the blame on Doug. He and Frank passed a few words with Doug when he arrived at the ranch-

29

house, as they were heading out for the brush.'

'What made Doug head into the sun?' Joe Wallace posed the question.

'Because Will Schrieber came back from town late on the day Dave Caswall was killed with the news that Doug was bein' blamed,' Ormond replied. 'We reckoned he'd best get to heck out of it until tempers cooled down an' folk started lookin' further than their noses. Doug left the same night.'

'And planning on joining the drive somewhere on the way to St Louis eh?' Travis said quickly. The ramrod and girl exchanged glances, but said nothing.

'The way I see it,' Joe Wallace said, slowly, 'is you either think Doug Machin is innocent an' needs help, or you're not sure an' you've gotta leave him to chance his luck with the law or a bounty-hunter. Wa'al, you make up yore minds. To do the best for an innocent man in his position you'd best confide in us; we'll make our own judgement an' it's more'n likely we'll keep him free while we look for the truth.'

Travis nodded to set the seal on Joe's statement, and, after a quick look at Ormond, Sally Machin stood up, and spoke with feeling. 'We know Doug's innocent; gunning someone down in cold blood isn't his style, but once he knows that his life's on the line because some killer bounty-hunter's on his

30

trail, he'll be a different proposition altogether. He can look out for himself, an' nobody's going to find him an easy mark.'

Neither Travis nor Wallace made an immediate reply as they came to their feet and reached for their hats; they were almost at the door when Joe Wallace turned around and gave the girl a straight look.

'I guess we understand yore problem, Ma'am. No sister worth her salt could hand her brother over to lawmen without talking it over first, an' without bein' sure it was in his best interests. Just remember, Caswall's killing isn't our assignment; we're just passing through with time to kill. We're interested on account that we don't much like bounty-hunters, an' a hombre in Springfield who marshal Travis rates as four-square, one Luke Withers, doesn't believe Doug Machin killed Caswall.'

Sally Machin's eyes lit up, and a smile showed briefly through her worry. 'Yeah, Luke would know; he's been a friend a long time. Most anyone you'd ask in Springfield would tell you the same.'

Both lawmen nodded and went out onto the verandah. Ormond followed close behind them. 'I'll get yore cayuses,' he said, 'then I'm gonna have this hyar range combed for Hanney. No bounty-hunter's gonna lie in wait anywhere on the Lazy Y to pick anybody off. We'll flush him out wherever he is.'

'Find him by all means, Ormond; even let him know you're watching him, but don't move him around any.'

Carl Travis gave the ramrod a hard look as he spoke. 'You prod him, an' he's got a cast-iron excuse to cut you down. We're gonna take a look at the Flying Diamond outfit, talk to those Caswall brothers, an' tomorrow we'll be back; then Hanney'll be our concern. He'd like fine to stop us interfering, but we're the law, United States law, and even Hanney'll think twice before getting the wrong side of it.'

'Yeah, mebbe you're right,' Hank Ormond admitted. 'Still, when you look in tomorrow I should be able to show you where he is.' With that he stepped off the verandah and made his way to the stables, leaving the lawmen to roll cigarettes and while the time away smoking.

A little later they rode to the south-west, the quickest route to the Flying Diamond, as directed by Hank Ormond. They were thoughtful for a time as they mulled over what the ramrod and Sally Machin had said, then Carl Travis moved Red closer alongside Wallace and glanced across at his deputy's face, now clear of concentration.

'Wa'al, Joe. What do you think?'

Joe's face split into one of his grins. 'I reckon it'd be better if you aired what you've been thinking,' he said. 'But for what it's worth, I think that Hank Ormond isn't too pleased that Miss Sally is close enough to Clem Caswall to have been considering getting wed before the old man got killed. If the accusation against her brother sticks, or if Hanney kills him covered by Sheriff Caswall's "dead or alive" dodger, then it's not likely the girl would marry into the Caswall family; an' judging by the fact Miss Sally wasn't keen on Ormond risking his neck with Hanney, it shows she likes him enough to give him a chance for a share in the Lazy Y.'

Travis gazed at the youngster in surprise. He knew Joe was picking things up pretty well, but this was deeper than he expected.

'I'd go along with the reasoning, Joe; there's mebbe just one thing wrong with it.'

'Yeah, I know,' Joe answered readily. 'While it's all true, Ormond doesn't seem that sort of schemer. He seems more likely to stay close to the girl no matter what, just to look out for her.'

They relapsed into silence for a while until they reached a summit, where they reined in and quartered the terrain. The Lazy Y ranch-house was in clear view, and as they watched, about twenty riders rode out of the compound, then separated, heading for the major points of the compass. Their purpose was obvious to the lawmen; Ormond had the search under way for Hanney.

'I've got a feeling, Joe, that Hanney is due

to be outsmarted for once. He's gonna be ringed by Lazy Y punchers no matter where he moves,' Carl Travis observed. 'I can't see Ormond letting him off the hook when he's got him tree'd.'

'Yeah, it looks that way,' Joe agreed. 'It also proves the Lazy Y hands are ready to back Ormond's opinion that Doug Machin's no killer.'

'I wouldn't go that far,' Carl demurred. 'It just proves nobody likes a bounty-hunter, an' Hanney less than most.'

Joe Wallace gave Travis an appreciative glance as they set off again. He could always depend upon the Marshal opening further avenues of thought. As they crossed onto Flying Diamond territory both men took careful stock of the terrain, memorizing every feature that could be used as a landmark.

Now and again riders showed up in the distance as they topped ridges. It was good, rolling grassland, broken here and there by rugged, stark hills beyond humped foothills, and a slow-running stream twisted its way from the rugged hills through miles of Flying Diamond land and onto the Lazy Y on its way to join the Cimarron River.

Each rider paused to watch the lawmen for a few minutes, then moved away on his own business when still too far away for recognition; then, with the Flying Diamond headquarters showing briefly in the distance through a gap, a rider moved out of cover at the foot of the hillside and sat waiting for them.

Sheriff Caswall nodded coolly as they reined in, his cold eyes roving from one to another. 'I thought you hombres would have moved on by now; ain't nothing I know to keep you here.'

'We're in no hurry, Sheriff,' Wallace said with a grin. 'It's mighty purty country an' we're lucky we've got some time to spare. It just could be you'll be seeing a lot more of us.'

A deep frown settled on Jake Caswall's face; then a sneer edged his lips. 'Well, suit yore-selves,' he said. 'Stay long enough an' you'll see Hanney bring in the killer, Machin, draped over his bronc.'

Neither man thought Caswall's statement worthy of comment, and they gigged their mounts forward, passing one each side of the hostile man. Savagely he slewed his mount and followed them. He was just behind them as they reined in underneath the verandah of the Flying Diamond ranch-house.

THREE

It was noticeable that none of the punchers outside the bunkhouse, and along the rails of the corral, exchanged words with the sheriff or gave any show of greeting. He pulled up his mount and tied it to the hitch-rail, and bounded up the five steps; pushed his way into the house, slamming the door behind him, and practically in Joe Wallace's face.

Joe eyed his companion and shrugged before thumping on the door. There was a two or three-minute interval when they could hear voices inside the house; then the door opened, and a tall, flashily dressed young man gazed at them out of narrowed eyes. His buckskin jacket was heavily fringed and generously decorated with rhinestones, and his calf-length, black-leather boots shone like glass. He took in their badges at one glance and addressed Travis as the senior.

'What can I do for you, Marshal?' he asked in a slow, lazy manner.

'I reckon it depends who you are,' Travis said pointedly. 'If you're one of the Caswall brothers then I guess we'd like to step inside and ask a few questions.'

The man nodded, his gaze sharpening, then he stepped aside. 'Come right on in, Marshal; I'm Clem Caswall.' Then, when Travis and Wallace had moved inside the house, he pointed to the two men standing in front of a big open fireplace, 'an that's Frank an' Sam. Jake I guess you've already met.'

Travis spared a glance at the sheriff, who was sitting alongside a table busily refilling his glass out of a bottle; then turned and nodded to the brothers. 'I'm Marshal Travis and this is Deputy Marshal Wallace.' He paused and looked at the brothers in turn. Their expressions gave nothing away; they just waited for him to continue. 'We were passing through when we heard about your father being killed. In the normal way, not being on a case, we'd have telegraphed our office and gotten permission to look into things, but we found Sheriff Caswall's brought in bounty-hunter Hanney. Well, we're on our own time for a few days, an' not liking bounty-hunters we've decided to spend the time looking into things.'

Sheriff Caswall snorted his annoyance, then pushed his chair away and stood up noisily. He glared at the lawmen before tossing down his drink, then with savagery in his voice, snarled: 'You can look all you want, Travis, but you're not wastin' my time. My money's on Hanney doin' the chore in double quick time.' With that he stumped angrily out of the house, and a moment later they heard him riding away.

Frank Caswall moved away from the fireplace and motioned the lawmen to seats at the long table. 'Make yoreselves comfortable and take yoreselves a drink,' he said, 'and ask any questions you want. I guess Jake's a bit touchy because we none of us thought calling in Hanney was a good idea. Jake did it before we had a chance to talk him out of it. We'd have sorted things out ourselves.'

'That's so,' Sam Caswall said from his place at the fireside.

As the lawmen helped themselves to a drink they covertly studied the Caswall brothers. Frank and Sam seemed cast out of the same mould. Swash-buckling, husky men with dark, homely features and crinkly, brown hair; they gave the look of living for a good time. Clem looked more calculating. Clem Caswall poured out drinks for himself and his brothers, and while Sam took his over to the fireplace, the other two sat opposite Travis and Wallace.

They all took a sip at their drinks and the brothers looked towards Travis, waiting for him to pose his questions. They seemed surprised when Joe Wallace spoke up: 'Perhaps you'll tell us everything you remember about the day your father was killed. That way it could save a lot of questions.'

Frank and Clem looked towards Sam to

39

start things going, and without hesitation he nodded. 'Wa'al, it needed 'bout an hour an' a half to sun-up when Ike Daley, Cal Smart an' me set off with the wagon for town. We gave Frank, Clem an' the boys a call as we left. We didn't hurry none an' arrived in town just when Mike Oakham was openin' up. We loaded up an' took a drink in the Panhandle before headin' home. I guess it was near midday when we got back, an' when Daley an' Smart got ready to start off-loadin' I went into the house.' Sam Caswall's face contorted for a moment as he brought the scene back into focus. 'The old man was slumped face down on the table, an' when my eyes got used to the change in light I could see a big stain on the boards under his feet. When I got to him I knew he was dead. I went to the door an' called in Daley an' Smart. We checked that he was dead an' carried him to that couch,' nodding to the leather settle that lay alongside the middle wall, 'an' covered him over.' He rubbed his hand over his chin, and there was anger in his face as he continued: 'There were two big holes in his stomach. He didn't stand a chance. I reckon the old man deserved better than that.' He paused. 'Wa'al, I sent Daley an' Smart to search the outbuildings while I took a look around the house, but we found nothing, so I sent Daley to tell Jake, an' Smart to let Frank an' Clem know. That's about all I guess. Jake got here first, an' a couple of hours later Frank an' Clem.'

Joe nodded, then looked across the table to the others. Frank pushed his drink away. 'Not much more to tell,' he said. 'We left Ike Holland to clear the brush of rogue steers, an' hightailed home. Sam an' Jake were here, Jake breathin' fire like always. We got talking things over, trying to piece together what might have happened, an' I remembered Doug Machin ridin' in just when we were leavin'. Jake got up an' left at that, an' I thought he was ridin' over to the Lazy Y to ask Doug if he'd seen any riders hanging around when he left, but he went straight back to town an' sent a telegraph to Hanney, naming Doug as the killer. We went over to the Lazy Y the next morning to ask Doug how he had left pa, but he'd lit out. Seems Will Schreiber got back from town late an' told Doug that the talk all over town was that he was bein' blamed for pa's killing, an' that the bounty-hunter, Hanney was booked to bring him in.'

'Yeah, I guess that about says it all,' Clem Caswall remarked when Frank sat back and reached for his drink.

'Anything stolen?' Joe asked, and the three brothers looked at each other uncertainly.

'Can't rightly say,' Frank said. 'Everything in the house seems to be in place. Only thing is, there's none of us know what

41

money pa kept in his safe. He never kept us short of dinero once we'd grown up – we got our shares without askin' – but he looked after the business end. I guess I never saw the inside of his safe from one year's end to another.'

'Yeah, we looked in the safe.' Sam broke in. 'When Jake came in from town he picked the key off the floor, an' later we all took a look. There's plenty of dinero in it, so it looks like nothing was stolen.'

'Do you know why Doug Machin called that morning?' Joe asked.

'Yeah,' Clem stated. 'Miss Sally an' Hank Ormond told us when we called at the Lazy Y next morning. Doug was offering to take a thousand of our steers on their drive to St Louis.'

'Can't see anything there to fight over,' Travis put in quietly.

'Nope, not on the face of it,' Clem agreed. 'There's just one thing though. Pa never sat at that table except when paying out dinero. He was mebbe paying Doug out a share of the drive costs an' provisioning.' He pointed to the big leather armchair at the opposite side of the fireplace from where Sam stood. 'If he sat anywhere it was on that chair, but he mostly stood alongside the fireplace an' leaned on the shelf. If you look, he's worn a groove on the end of that shelf.'

'Did your father give any of you a hard

time?' Joe asked.

The three brothers shook their heads, and Frank said without hesitation: 'He brought us up on a tight lead, but he didn't cow us any, an' when we got as good as the next man he gave us our heads. I guess it was only Jake who rubbed him the wrong way. It was just that Jake didn't care much for punchin' cattle, an' when the chance came to take the sheriff's job Jake didn't waste any time.'

'I reckon yore pa sounds like he'd keep tight records of everything,' Carl Travis interposed. 'Mebbe one of you could take a look through an' check out the dinero in the safe.' Then, after a pause: 'I'd lend a hand if you'd like.'

Frank and Clem looked towards Sam, who nodded his agreement. He went over to the bureau, took out a small key from the first drawer, then pulled aside a big sketch picture of a herd of horses to reveal a safe, which he opened. He took out a large tin box and handed it to Clem, then handed some ledgers to Frank and brought over a couple more. With cash-box and ledgers on the table Frank poured out drinks for everybody, and passed around a tobacco jar and papers.

While they rolled smokes Joe leaned over towards the brothers, his face serious. 'Do you think Doug Machin could've killed yore father in cold blood?'

Frank Caswall's brown eyes brooded for a full minute before he replied. 'If we believed that, one hundred percent, Marshal Wallace, we'd be turnin' over every blade of grass searchin' for him, an' we wouldn't let up until we had him strung from the nearest tree. But we've known Doug a long time, an' we find it hard to believe. It seems Jake's a hundred percent sure, an' being the lawman, he's got a right to bring in Hanney. I guess we don't know what to think, now that Doug's rode into the sun.'

'One thing's for sure,' Clem Caswall put in. 'There's nothin' hot-tempered 'bout Doug Machin, so if he did the killing, it was deliberate. I guess I'd like to know.' The man's remarks seemed to hang in the air for a long time until Sam started to shuffle the ledgers around.

Sam then opened the cash-box and pushed it towards Travis and Joe. 'Mebbe you'd like to count that while I set these in order?'

Travis reached over and overturned the box, leaving the piles of neatly banded notes on the table; then, spreading them out, sorted them in denominations, and started in to count each bundle. He wrote on the last note the figure in each bundle and passed the bundles to Joe who agreed the amounts shown in each bundle. At the end they counted $10,500.

The ledgers proved no problem. Dave Caswall had kept clear records of every transaction he had made. There was a ledger for each of his four sons, showing every last dollar he had paid them over the last ten years. Each son had been paid according to his age and experience, until in the last couple of years, Sam, Frank and Clem were paid the same and their accredited shares in the assets of the Flying Diamond were the same. Jake's ledger showed no payment for the last six months, and for the period before, since he presumably became sheriff, he had received half of what the other brothers took, and his share of the assets remained stagnant from that time. The main ledger was a model of simplicity, and showed assets in Springfield Bank of $220,000 and cash at $12,500.

Travis made sure that Joe studied each ledger carefully; then, when satisfied that his deputy had taken in all of the implications of the figures, he looked at the brothers one after another, and asked: 'Any of you taken anything out've that box since your father's death?'

They shook their heads in time with each other.

'Right! Then we know that it's $2,000 light,' Travis said. 'If Machin was taking a thousand head of steers for the Flying Diamond do you reckon that sum would have covered provisioning and expenses?'

45

Frank shrugged his shoulders. 'I wouldn't know, but five years ago we took a thousand head for the Lazy Y; mebbe the ledger'll show what Frank Machin paid the old man.'

Travis reached for the ledger and turned back the pages, but he could find no entry of payment by Frank Machin. He passed the ledger back to the brothers. 'Wa'al, it seems no money changed hands on account of moving their steers, so I'd think Doug Machin was about to return the favour.'

'Mebbe Doug asked for the dinero anyways,' Clem suggested, 'an' the old man got hot under the collar and gave his opinion of Doug in the way that gets most folk hoppin' mad.'

Neither Sam nor Frank made any comment, so Travis stood up and Joe Wallace untangled his long legs and followed suit.

'We're obliged for answering our questions,' Carl said, 'an' we'll look into things. If Doug Machin is guilty we'll bring him in, but he'll have a fair trial.'

'Unless Hanney gets to him first,' Sam Caswall muttered. 'It's beginning to look to me like Machin is guilty, an' I don't care overmuch if Hanney does get to him.' Clem and Frank didn't add anything, but their expressions showed they were inclined to Sam's opinion.

The brothers drew together, wanting to talk over the possibilities of the killing having arisen from Doug Machin's demand for payment for including the Flying Diamond steers, and they hardly noticed the lawmen make their exit. Travis and Wallace untied their cayuses and, climbing into their saddles, headed away on the trail to town.

Some time later they sat at a table away from the crowd in the Panhandle saloon, replete after a good meal and eyeing their brimming glasses of beer with anticipation. As they rolled smokes a bevy of women pushed through the batwing doors and stared around the occupied tables. Just behind them came Sheriff Caswall, his face showing signs of heavy drinking. There were calls of invitation to the women from all quarters, and, as they made their choices, Jake Caswall grabbed the arm of a big, blonde, busty woman and led her to a table at the opposite side of the room.

The barkeep served him first, bringing a bottle of corn whisky and another of gin together with glasses. Caswall paid from a thick roll of notes that had the blonde pulling her chair close to him.

'I don't reckon that hombre's in the same class as his brothers,' Joe muttered, after taking a pull at his beer.

Carl Travis smiled.

'No, you're mebbe right. Mind, they're none of 'em angels, and nary a one would stand away from a fight. I guess the other three get all they want without pushing any, on account of 'em bein' born cattle-handlers an' having been raised by a man who saw value in that. They've found all they want close to home, an' the old man kept 'em happy by giving 'em shares of the profits on top of top-hand pay.'

Joe Wallace nodded before taking another large swallow out of his glass; then, as though thinking aloud, said: 'I'd have thought that if old man Caswall had given Machin that $2,000 he'd have asked for a receipt for the money, especially as when he did the same favour no money passed between 'em.'

'Nope!' Carl said emphatically. 'They might have taken account of that by Caswall giving the Machins a lower price per head, or showing a lesser number of beeves sold under Machin's brand.'

Joe took a long time considering this, his eyes on Sheriff Caswall's slobbering advances to the big blonde. 'So, the old man might have had cause to fly off the handle if Machin had asked him to fork out before the drive for provisions an' other expenses,' he said at length.

'Yeah, an' old Dave would have lumped it all in with what he paid into the bank,' Carl remarked.

'Well, what d'you reckon we ought to do next?' Joe asked, before draining his glass and crossing to the counter to fetch two more. Having set down the refills he waited for Travis to expound.

'Like I said, Joe, this is your case, an' I'm leaving you in town to take care of it.' Carl watched the doubts flit across Joe's big, homely face before the calm returned, then added: 'I'm going to make sure that Hanney doesn't fill young Machin full of lead before he gets the chance of a trial, so as soon as I can get some provisions together I'll be headin' for the Lazy Y.'

Joe Wallace's big smile spread over his face. 'I'll sleep easier knowing you're keeping tabs on that Hanney hombre; but just one thing before you light out, let's go over everything the Caswalls had to say, an' talk about those ledgers again.'

They spent an hour going over everything and Joe made notes with a stub of pencil as points struck him, and by the time he stuffed the sheaf of papers back into his pocket glimmerings of ideas were darting around his mind. Carl Travis did no more than recount the entire conversation with the Caswall brothers and mention every significant point about the ledgers. It was now up to Joe. He himself was about to ensure that no injustice would take place such as Machin's demise at the hands of Hanney, so if Joe came up against a brick wall nothing would be lost.

Carl Travis rode out of town a little later,

and Joe sought his bed in the Panhandle hotel. He lay awake for a long time, with the oil lamp burning full strength, making reference time and again to his notes, then after a final smoke he slept the sleep of the innocent, content in the belief that he knew what he had to do.

FOUR

Travis arrived at the Lazy Y without challenge, and guessed that most hands were out keeping tabs on Hanney. He tied Red to the hitchrail and clumped noisily up the steps to the verandah. As he got to the door he could hear low voices from inside; then a door opened and shut. He knocked hard and deliberately, and a minute later the door opened to the length of a chain, and Ormond, with gun in hand, peeked through the opening.

'You won't be needing that,' Travis said. 'I'd just like a talk with you an' Miss Sally.'

Hank Ormond holstered the gun and, releasing the chain, opened up for Travis to enter. When the lawman's eyes adjusted to the light he saw Sally Machin standing at the end of the table, a glass held in one hand and a Stetson in the other. He smiled inwardly as he noted she wore a neat, grey dress, and was in no way ready for riding; he doubted the Stetson would fit her anyway. She motioned him to a seat, and Ormond, following in, offered him a drink.

'We – er– We didn't expect to see you again so soon, Marshal Travis,' the girl said.

'What is it you want now?'

'Always the same thing, I guess,' Carl said. 'Some answers to questions. They keep cropping up and I get restless until I get the answers.'

'Well, you just put the questions, Marshal Travis, an' if we can answer 'em we will,' Ormond said as he pushed a drink across the table before sitting down.

Travis looked hard at Ormond and Sally Machin in turn, then shook his head. 'Nope, it's only Doug's got the answers I want, so you might as well let him come out from the back-room an' say his piece.'

Ormond's eyes narrowed, and he pushed back to go for his guns, but stopped with his hands in mid-air. Carl Travis had hardly appeared to move, but his gun was levelled at the ramrod's chest unwaveringly.

'Now that would've been real dumb, Ormond,' Carl observed. 'It wouldn't do anybody any good to shoot a lawman. If you want to help yore boss, you'd best call to him to come back for his Stetson, an' with his guns holstered.'

The connecting door opened, and a young, broad-shouldered man with the unmistakable Machin corn-gold hair and cobalt-blue eyes stepped into the room. He looked first at Sally and Ormond, shrugging his shoulders before taking stock of the lawman. 'I've heard what you've all said, Marshal Travis;

maybe you'll tell me how it's gonna help me to answer any of your questions.'

'Sure I'll tell you. If your answers tie in with what I think, then it'll help you to have me on Hanney's tail when you ride out. That'll keep you safe while my pard finds the answers to some other questions we've got. Mind, if you killed Dave Caswall I'd see you hang quite cheerfully after a proper trial.'

Doug Machin came around the table and poured himself a drink before sitting down, then methodically he rolled himself a smoke. Finally, he looked across at Travis. 'Ask yore questions, Marshal.'

Travis returned his gun to its holster and looked at Ormond. 'I reckon you've got Hanney hemmed in somewhere.' And when the ramrod nodded, 'When I say, you can take the heat off him an' leave him to me.' Then he returned his attention to Doug Machin. 'Wa'al now, we've already asked questions over at the Flying Diamond, an' we've taken a look at the safe an' ledgers, so it's just straight answers I want.'

Machin's eyes widened. 'Am I supposed to have stolen something from the Caswalls as well as killin' old Dave?'

Travis ignored the question. 'Why did you call at the Flying Diamond?'

'To offer to take a thousand head of their beef with ours to St Louis.'

'Did Dave Caswall take you up on it?'

53

'Sure, an' why not. We were only makin' things even.'

'Did you have a drink with him?'

Doug Machin nodded. 'Yeah, I guess we had three or four before I left. Dave's allus been pretty free with it.'

'Where did you both sit at the long table with yore drinks?'

Machin laughed. 'I didn't sit. I stood one side of the fireplace an' Dave stood the other, like always.'

'You went to the table then when Dave paid you the expenses for the drive. Is that it?'

Machin's eyes widened. 'What expenses?' he barked. 'I never asked for any an' Dave didn't offer; that's not the way we work.'

Travis merely nodded. 'So neither you nor Dave sat at the table?'

'No! Why?' Doug's look was sharp.

'Where did you leave Dave when you rode home?' Travis asked.

'On the verandah. He turned back indoors just before I passed the end corral.'

Carl Travis sat upright and reached for his glass. Then he gazed frankly at the two men and girl, and his expression was kindly. 'Your answers convince me of something, Machin, an' that is a whole lot more investigating needs to be done before a bounty-hunter gets the right to take a bead on you. I'm surprised you went into hiding when Will Schrieber

54

brought the news from town, but I guess you know the Caswalls better than I do.' He paused, but the others said nothing, and he continued: 'If you're intending keeping out of Hanney's way, Machin, then you'd best get on the run, or else you're gonna get some hombre killed on yore account. Hanney's not gonna stay hemmed in for long.'

Machin shot a surprised look at the lawman, and Sally Machin showed concern.

'If Doug rides off, then I'm goin' with him,' Ormond said flatly. 'Nobody's gonna take him from the back.'

Travis shook his head. 'Nope. I'll be doggin' Hanney every step of the way, an' before Machin moves off we'll agree just where he'll travel, an' where he ends up. I've heard rumours about Hanney an' I'd like a chance of seein' where he steps outside the law.' He paused, then gave Ormond a straight look. 'I want you to take the notes which I'm gonna write of the questions an' answers that've just passed between Machin an' me to Deputy Marshal Wallace at Springfield. You'll find him most likely in the eatin'-house, the Panhandle saloon an' hotel, or just around town.'

Doug Machin looked squarely at Carl Travis, and the cobalt-blue eyes were steady. 'Y'know, Marshal, when it comes down to cases, Hanney don't scare me none. I know what I've done or not done, an' in my mind I've as much right to be gunnin' for Hanney as the other way round. Facin' up to things, he could find he's got no edge on me.'

'That's so, 'cept Hanney's got the law on his side fer now,' Carl said brusquely. As he spoke he pulled a notebook and pencil from his pocket and started writing in the questions and answers he wanted Joe to have, and ignored the others. He wasn't too absorbed, however, to miss the exchange of glances between the girl and her brother, which, summed up, pointed to acquiescence with his demands, nor to note an expression of annoyance fleet across Ormond's face, before his brow creased with concentrated thought.

'You'd better pack up enough chow to last me a few days, Sally,' Doug Machin said at length, 'then I'll head out.' He then directed his attention to Travis. 'Just one thing, Marshal; if that hombre Hanney gets close to me, then I'll see how good he is face to face. Right's on my side no matter what anyone says, an' no matter what you might think.'

Carl made no comment, but completed the notes and handed them to Hank Ormond. 'If you'll take these to Marshal Wallace first, you'll have time to pick me up here an' get me to where Hanney's hemmed in.'

Ormond looked towards Machin, his eyes rebellious, but Doug nodded before saying,

'As soon as Hanney's on the move you'd better get the herd rounded up for the drive, an' take over the Flying Diamond beef. Maybe by then everything will have sorted itself out; the critturs should be on the hoof in a couple of weeks.'

The ramrod stood up and stuck his hand out to clasp Doug's hand. 'I'll take care of things like you say; just you keep a sharp eye to yore back.'

Machin grinned back at Ormond, who stowed away the notes Travis handed to him, and headed out into the night after looking towards Sally Machin with undisguised longing. The girl's answering smile was no more than friendly.

Travis turned to Machin as Sally left the room to prepare the provisions Doug had requested. 'We'd better get down to cases, an' work out the route you'll take; whichever way you go I'd like to end up in Las Animas, which is Hanney's home territory. If he steps outside the line of the law, it's in Las Animas I'd like to nail him.'

Doug smiled, and went to a cabinet, returning with pencil and paper. Spreading the paper on the table he proceeded to draw an equilateral triangle with the apex at the bottom of the paper. At the bottom or south he marked in Springfield, then near the north-west angle, La Junta, at the north-east angle, Syracuse, and at the most northerly point, Lamar; then adding each side of Lamar, Granada and Holly, in the Syracuse direction, and Las Animas on the La Junta side. With swift strokes he filled in the topographical details and distances, even adding relative heights of peaks.

Carl watched him in open admiration. Machin was totally absorbed, and the lawman revised his opinion of the young rancher's chances of keeping Hanney at bay if left to fend for himself; any man with Machin's ability to memorise and sketch terrain so readily must also have a sharp awareness for every advantage the terrain offered.

Machin leaned back for a moment, studying his sketch; then he proceeded to fill in his intended route with thick dashes. When he finished he studied it again for at least three minutes, then handed the sketch to the lawman, who studied in turn.

'You're sure some artist,' Carl remarked at length. 'I reckon if you ever get fed up with runnin' a cattle-ranch the railway companies both east coast an' west coast would part with plenty dinero for yore services.'

'Y'know, Marshal Travis, if I could find a hombre who I could really trust to run this outfit an' look out for Sally, that's just where I'd be headin'.'

'What about Ormond?' Carl asked.

Doug Machin seemed to look inward for a long time before shaking his head. 'I ain't got cause to say no to that 'cept mebbe instinct. Nope, there's only one hombre who I'd trust, an' he's not able to fork a cayuse fer long these days; he's also busy with his father's affairs, so I guess I'll have to stay.'

'You mean Luke Withers, the livery-man?'

'Yeah, there's no hombre I know who measures up better'n Luke.'

Carl Travis nodded. He had been forming the opinion that Doug Machin was innocent of the charge levelled against him, and now the man's opinion of Luke Withers' virtues cemented the opinion into a belief. He, himself, had formed a high opinion of Withers.

Travis looked again at the map, then back at Machin. 'Just one thing. Hanney's not gonna be harin' after you; he'll travel at a steady pace. But one thing's for sure – he won't stop at sundown the first night. He'll use that time to get close, so that your trail shows up fresh. He'll mebbe only sleep 'bout three hours. That means you've got to travel all of thirty-six hours without sleep.'

'I'd already reckoned on that,' Machin replied. 'Sleep won't bother me none, I can manage seventy-two hours anytime, but I'll take two cayuses; no sense in takin' chances.'

With that Machin stood up and checked his guns, then from a drawer in the cabinet he collected a box of ammunition, and took down a Winchester rifle from the wall beside the cabinet. He checked it carefully, then placed it beside the ammunition and his

59

Stetson. With a sly grin at Travis he then extracted from the deep left-hand pocket of his buckskin jacket a tiny single-shot derringer, a devastating weapon at short range, and examined it thoroughly before replacing it in its pocket-holster.

'Wa'al, that's that I guess,' he said, as he poured himself a drink before passing the bottle to Carl and sitting down. 'Soon as Sally's got the chow ready an' the aparejos filled I'll get on my way.'

'I'll see you on yore way, then get what sleep I can in that deep chair until Ormond gets back,' Carl remarked.

'Sure thing,' Machin acquiesced; then both men became silent, and their chins sunk into their chests as they cat-napped comfortably.

It seemed just a few minutes later when Sally Machin came from the inner room carrying the saddlebags, stuffed with provisions, and two large aparejos containing water. Doug stood up straight away; then, taking the gear, he leaned down and kissed her on the forehead. Carl got up and moved around to take them from Machin, leaving him to bring his rifle, ammunition and saddle-roll.

'Now, don't fret none, Sal,' Doug said. 'I'll be back home again in no time, an' all this business will be behind us.'

The girl's eyes glistened, but she managed a smile.

'Yeah, sure you will, Doug. I'll find plenty to do in the meantime.'

Machin turned abruptly, and picking up the items from the table led the way to the door. Sally lowered the lamp to a pinpoint so when he opened the door no light spilled through, and he and Travis slipped out in the dark.

In the stables a couple of animals nickered, but for the most part the horses were quietly dozing. Doug led out a couple of cayuses from their stalls, and he and Travis saddled up one and fixed the lead rein on the other. The lawman left Machin to fix his gear on the saddled horse to suit his preferences, but out of interest he ran a practised hand over both animals to judge their suitability for the chore in hand. He reckoned Machin had made a good choice.

Doug led the animals outside; then with a quick shake of Travis' hand, he climbed into the saddle and rode off into the night, leaving Carl to return to the house to await Ormond.

Joe Wallace came awake at Ormond's first knock on his door, and with one fluid movement he grabbed his gun from under the pillow and slid out of bed. Ormond knocked again, and Joe called out: 'Who is it? An' what'n heck do you want?'

'It's Ormond, Marshal Wallace. I've got

some notes for you from Marshal Travis.'

Joe recognized the ramrod's voice and slipping into his Levis he crossed to the door and slipped the bolt; then he raised the lamp-wick, keeping his eye on the door. Hank Ormond pushed the door inward and stepped inside.

'You're lucky to have got yourself some sleep, Marshal,' Ormond said, with feeling. 'I'm missin' out on it on account Travis took advantage of my good nature.'

Joe grinned. 'He can be mighty persuasive when he's of a mind, but of one thing you can be sure: there's nothing he does that ain't worth the doin', an' that goes for anything he asks anyone else to do. Seein' he's lookin' out for young Machin, then you've probably been helpin' out yore boss.'

There was little show of enthusiasm from Ormond as he dug into his inside pocket and withdrew Travis' notes. He handed them to Joe, and his look was sour. 'I'm not so sure I wouldn't be doing Doug a better favour by doggin' Hanney myself instead of leavin' it to Travis.'

Joe placed the notes alongside the lamp and gave the ramrod his full attention. 'Yeah, I understand just how you feel,' he said. 'No doubt you'd keep tabs on Hanney as well as any other hombre, but when it comes to, Hanney'd still have the law on his side. Another thing, who'd be lookin' after Machin's interests in the Lazy Y?'

Ormond seemed to consider this; then his disgruntled expression cleared, and he buttoned up his jacket. 'Well, I'll leave you to chew over those notes, an' I'll get back to yore boss.' Then with a nod he passed through the door, closing it behind him. Joe rolled himself a cigarette and smoked his way through it before slipping out of his Levis and getting back between the sheets.

For the best part of an hour he read and re-read the questions Travis had posed and the answers he had received, until he knew them off by heart, but nothing came to him in a sudden illuminating flash, so he composed himself for sleep with the intention of giving them more thought after a few more hours in bed and a stimulating meal at the eating-house.

Sleep didn't come so easily. As he sank into comatose comfort a point would jump out at him and he'd be wide awake, worrying over the implications, and most of the remaining night slipped away with Joe's grey matter working overtime. When he woke up for the last time and slid his long frame out of bed, the assertion by Doug Machin that he and Dave Caswall had not sat at the table was branded on his brain.

He built himself a smoke and allowed the thoughts to chase around in his mind. All of the Caswall brothers had agreed that Dave

63

Caswall had died whilst sat at the table, yet the fact niggled that they could be in collusion. Then he remembered Sam Caswall had stated he had called in Daley and Smart immediately after finding his father dead – they had helped him move the corpse to the sofa. Then he remembered Jake Caswall had picked the safe key from the floor upon entry into the house. Why had the key escaped Sam Caswall and the two hands? Was it because the sheriff had been at the ranch earlier and helped himself to the $2,000 that were missing, and had forgotten the key in his hurry to get away.

Joe kept his mind on that tack. Jake Caswall was the only brother who seemed to have a genuine cause for killing his father. Six months had gone by without a single dollar being handed to him, whilst his brothers were paid good bonuses on top of top-hand pay. The man's nature was grasping, that was for sure, and he looked like a man who would worry at a grudge until it became obsessional. Then Joe remembered the thickness of the roll Jake Caswall had flashed in front of the big blonde in the saloon. 'Yeah,' he said to himself. 'That hombre needs checking out.'

After a good wash in the cold water in the big washbowl Joe reached for his Stetson and made his way to the eating-house, where he ordered double portions of everything, and drank a couple of mugs of coffee while waiting for it to be cooked.

He was halfway through his meal when a tall, dark-haired, handsome man made his way through the door, limping heavily. The newcomer had nearly closed the distance before Joe recognized him as the livery-man who had taken care of their cayuses the first night they had arrived in Springfield. The man was dressed neatly in black jacket, white shirt and black string tie, with black Levis, and angle-length black boots. He had thick, curly hair, and his eyes crinkled in the corners as his face split in a smile of recognition.

'Mind if I join you?' he asked, as he limped to a stop.

'I'd sure welcome yore company,' Joe replied, giving the big grin that lit his face like a sunrise. 'Pack yore freight.'

Luke Withers sat down opposite Joe, favouring his left leg carefully. Joe kept up his attack on his breakfast with total enjoyment, but his one eye was appraising the other man.

'We didn't get to introductions the night you hit town,' Withers said, 'but I got to talkin' to Marshal Travis when he collected yore cayuse yesterday. My moniker's Luke Withers.'

Joe thrust a horny hand across the table. 'Glad to know you, Luke. I'm Joe Wallace. I guess I'll order up some more chow to keep you company, then mebbe you'll fill me in with anything you know about the folk of Springfield.'

'Be glad to,' Withers replied, then when the little Chinaman came alongside he gave him his full attention. 'Howdy, Lin San. I guess I'll have the usual, an' I reckon the Marshal could manage another plate of what he fancies.'

FIVE

With their meal finished, and a large coffee-pot set between them, the two men built themselves cigarettes and spread themselves comfortably.

'Marshal Travis handed on all that passed between you an' him,' Joe said at length, 'an' the one thing that sticks in my mind is that you don't rate Doug Machin as a cold-blooded killer.'

'Yeah, that's so, Joe. And, anyway, I wouldn't know of any reason why Doug an' Dave Caswall would fall out to cause either of 'em to go for their guns. They've allus got on fine. Dave's been an ornery cuss most of his life but it's never been more than his bark, unless any hombre tried stealin' his stock or creepin' onto his graze. His bark was enough to keep his sons in line until he gave them their heads, an' before he got killed he knew that the spadework on the ranch could be left to 'em. He liked 'em to enjoy 'emselves in town, an' to be as pushy as they wanted. Between Frank, Sam an' Clem roisterin' around, and Jake bein' sheriff, Dave had Springfield all sewn up. He never pushed any of the traders, so I guess there were very few men in Springfield who bore him any grudges.'

'How 'bout the Machins and the Caswalls; there's not much difference in the size of their spreads; how've they got on over the years?'

'Never any trouble between 'em, 'cept the old ruckus now an' again between the hands. Still, old man Machin an' Dave Caswall were buddies from way back an' arrived on this range together with a hundred steers between 'em. They married a couple of girls from Wichita Falls who'd been friends for years, so there was never much chance of the families warring. Mrs Caswall died, together with the Machins, when a part of the trail collapsed into the Canadian River just north of the Panhandle, taking their stage with it. They were making a visit to Wichita. That was just over five years ago.'

Joe nodded, then thinking of Jake Caswall and the roll of banknotes he'd sported, 'How about the sheriff, Jake Caswall. What can you say about him?'

Luke Withers took a long time to answer. 'Jake's never been popular with anyone. He's allus been quick-tempered, an' too fond of the bottle. Treats women like dirt; can't tell a decent girl from the sort that sells themselves. He got his marchin' orders from the Machins on account of that.' A dark flush settled on Withers' face as he dragged the memory from the past. 'I guess he's been as jealous as all heck of Clem these last coupla years.'

Joe Wallace digested the information, but didn't press his companion to elaborate on the theme. It was apparent to him that Luke Withers set a great deal of score on Sally Machin. Remembering the limp that hampered Withers' movement, Joe concluded that the disability mattered enough to prevent him pressing his own case with the girl. Joe decided to pose another question, however, that Withers would probably prefer not to answer.

'How about the ramrod, Hank Ormond. How does he get on with the Caswalls? I reckon he's mighty protective of Miss Sally, an' I don't think it's just on account he ramrods the spread. Any bad blood between him an' Clem Caswall?'

Luke Withers' face was burning again, and there was anger in his grey eyes. When he answered, however, he was under control. 'If there's any bad blood between 'em, they keep it to themselves. I reckon Ormond keeps his place when Clem's around, although good as Clem is with the hardware I reckon Ormond'd have the edge on him. Anyway, I guess Clem knows that as well as anybody. All the Caswalls, an' Doug an' me, were in the Panhandle saloon about three years ago when Billy Shanklin rode into town threatenin' to ventilate anyone who stood in his way. Shanklin sure had one heck of a reputation an' nobody was pushing to be his next gun notch. Then in came Ormond.' Withers paused to savour the memory before continuing.

'Well, Shanklin settled on Ormond, an' goaded him into going for his irons. That half a minute when they sized each other an' tried to impose their will on the other lasted like all of time. Shanklin moved first, but he kept movin' an' finished up face down in the sawdust. When they turned him over he had two holes close together in his forehead. Ormond didn't turn a hair; killing a hombre didn't seem to bother him none.'

'You've given me plenty to mull over, Luke,' Joe Wallace said, with a smile. 'I'm mighty obliged to you.'

Withers stood up and thrust some coins into Lin San's hand, who stood alongside. Wallace followed suit. 'I'll walk you back,' he said, and Withers nodded his thanks.

Together they made their way to the livery where a smart-looking buggy stood outside and a tow-headed youngster leaned against the wall soaking up the sun. Seeing them, the youngster disappeared inside to reappear with a well-muscled Appaloosa, which he proceeded to hitch up to the buggy.

'I'm drivin' out to the Lazy Y,' Withers remarked as they drew close to the buggy. 'I want to know what the score is from Sally, an' see if there's any help I can give.' Then, when Wallace just nodded, he turned to the youngster. 'Thanks, Seth. If you get any problems roust the old man out, he'll sort 'em.'

'Don't worry, Luke, there's nothin' here I can't handle.'

'No, I guess not. Er, meet Marshal Wallace.' And turning to Joe, 'Seth Paget. He lends a hand whenever I want. There's nothing he don't know about horseflesh, but he's gonna waste his time goin' east soon to learn to be a banker.'

The marshal and Seth Paget shook hands solemnly as Luke Withers climbed aboard with some difficulty. Then with a shake of the reins the Appaloosa moved off smartly, and Luke gave them a wave.

'Well, I sure wish you luck when you go east, Seth. I reckon there's more reward in banking than wet-nursing cayuses.'

Seth's eyes clouded. 'I guess I'll only use the dinero to surround myself with the critturs,' he said. Joe grinned as he turned away, and as he rounded the end of Main Street he gave the youngster a wave.

'Marshal Travis decided not to wait for you to come back, Hank,' Sally Machin said as Ormond pushed into the big living room. 'He said for you to tell Hanney he's free to

71

go whichever way he likes, an' for you not to dog him when he leaves his hide-out.'

Hank Ormond found difficulty in containing his temper. He poured himself a stiff drink and walked around the room, taking in the paper-ash in the open fireplace and Doug's sketching pad on the top of the cabinet. Sally Machin watched the ramrod for a minute or so, then muttering about making coffee she went into the kitchen. Ormond went immediately to the sketch-pad and, picking it up, held it to the lamp. He remembered that Doug pressed hard when drawing, but the paper showed no indentations. The ash in the fireplace told its own story. The ramrod cursed to himself: the blamed marshal trusted no-one.

He built himself a smoke to go along with the drink, and drew deep pulls of the acrid tobacco into his lungs. When Sally re-entered the room, bearing a tray loaded with coffee and mugs, he was hard put to clear the scowl of frustration from his face.

'Get yoreself outside some hot coffee before you go out again, Hank,' she said. 'The longer you take to get to Hanney, the more time Doug's got to get on his way.'

'Yeah, I reckon you're right,' he replied, stopping his pacing and taking a seat. 'I sure hope Travis is as good a tracker as he makes out. I'd have liked it better if I'd ridden out right alongside Doug.' He paused, giving her time to express an opinion, but the girl said nothing. 'Did Doug say which way he'd be headin'?' he asked at length.

'No.' She gave him a frank look. 'I guess that was between the marshal and Doug. They purposely didn't tell me.'

Ormond drank down the scalding liquid, then stood up. 'I'll mosey on out an' take the ring of men that're holding Hanney away. Are you sure you wouldn't prefer that I trailed him, just to keep Doug sure, certain safe?'

Sally Machin thought over his question a long time, and differing emotions showed on her face as the thoughts raced, then she gave him that straight, steady look that bothered him. 'It's not what I'd prefer, Hank. It's just gotta be like Doug says, an' he goes along with what Marshal Travis says. If there's any back-up necessary, that young Marshal Wallace could well be providing it. Anyways, Hank, Doug wants you to get the round-up done so that the drive'll be ready to roll when the trouble sorts itself out.'

The ramrod expelled his breath in an exasperated way, then forced a smile onto his lips. He picked up his Stetson, and after nodding to the girl, made his way outside and rode away.

Just an hour later, he made contact with Smiley, the first puncher who by daylight had a bead on Moss Hanney. He passed the word for him to call the others off, and to make as much noise as they liked as they rode away. As Smiley saddled up his cayuse Ormond slid to the ground and prepared to wait for daybreak. 'Get 'em all back to the bunkhouse an' get plenty of shuteye,' he said to Smiley. 'About mid-day we'll be headin' out to dig out mavericks from wherever they're hiding.'

When Smiley rode away, Ormond's mind was working overtime. He had to let things take their course as the way stood, because there was just no way he could get into the action without going against those pesky US marshals. It was several smokes later, with the first feint of dawn showing in the east, that the way to handle things came to him. His first move was to get Hanney riled.

Moving out from cover as the light strengthened, he stared towards the spot Hanney had chosen to keep tabs on the Lazy Y, and soon he saw smoke rising from a newly started fire. A little later the stirring morning air brought the tang of coffee to him. Ormond stood up and, cupping his mouth with his hands, shouted.

'Hey! Hanney! This is Ormond, ramrod of this outfit! I want to palaver with you.'

'Say yore piece, Ormond, an' fork yore freight!' The harsh metallic voice cut through the air like a whiplash.

'Nope, I'll come down!' Ormond shouted.

'Ain't no sense in bein' at loggerheads.'

'Aw, suit yourself!' the answer came back. 'Just keep yore hands where I can see 'em. First fancy move an' yore dead!'

Ormond smiled to himself, and swinging into the saddle rode into the open and took a route that brought him into Hanney's immediate view. The bounty-hunter stood beside his fire, the long ankle-length coat open and pulled back, showing the twin Colts handy in their tied-down holsters. As Ormond got close he felt the power of the man's black, glittering eyes, but he didn't respond to the projected menace of Hanney's stance and hypnotic gaze.

The ramrod stopped a few yards away and dropped out of the saddle to stand relaxed, his eyes on the hanging coffee pot. 'Smells mighty good,' he drawled. 'Enough there for two?'

Hanney laughed mirthlessly. 'Yeah, it'll stretch for two, just so long as you don't mind usin' the same mug that three stiffs last used.'

Ormond shrugged. 'It all depends whether it was lead poisonin' that killed 'em or yore coffee.'

Moss Hanney didn't bother to answer, but crossed to his gear and pulled out the other mug, at the same time keeping an eye on the ramrod. He placed the mug alongside his own, then stood away from the fire. 'You fill 'em up,' he ordered. Then, as Ormond leaned over the fire to fill the mugs, 'So judgin' from the noise yore men made when they moved out, Machin's made his break, an' you're reckoning on him havin' enough start to keep a whole skin.'

Ormond shook his head. 'He's on the hoof now right enough, but he's got no worries 'bout you catchin' up with him. Machin's no ordinary hombre, Hanney. No sirree. He'll lead you up blind alleys an' false trails until you're dizzy, an' more often than not he'll have you in his sights. By day an' night there'll be times when he could leave you for buzzard meat. Even if he lets you come face to face he'll beat you to the draw.'

Moss Hanney picked up the mug Ormond set down, and moved away with it to sit on a boulder. 'I guess you're trying to do the best for yore boss, Ormond, but it cuts no ice. The moment I get astride that crittur an' set off after Machin he's as good as dead.'

'You'll have to salivate him on first sight from a distance, Hanney, if you get that lucky. There's no other way you'll beat him.' Ormond made it sound matter of fact. 'He's convinced Marshal Travis he don't need wet-nursing. Anyway, Travis is movin' out.'

Hanney's eyes glittered as he stared at Ormond. 'It's never been my policy to take any notice of reputations passed on from mouth to mouth. I only know what I can do, an' I'm satisfied that Machin'll cause me no more trouble than any of the others I got paid for.'

'I can prove to you Machin's special right now, Hanney,' Ormond snapped, and now his face was hard. 'You're unlucky that you hit a neck of the woods where two men can beat you to the draw any time you like. Machin's the fastest; the other's me.'

As he spoke Ormond moved his hands slowly, thumbs and forefingers extended, and gingerly picked his guns out of their holsters. He swung them a couple of times and let go so that they landed at Hanney's feet. 'Unload 'em, an' toss 'em back, and you can go for the hardware when you like.'

Hanney glanced down at the guns before turning his chilling look at Ormond. 'The only time I go for my guns, Ormond, is when it's for keeps. I'll never play games to prove who clears leather first. It don't signify much anyway. It's who gets the first shot to the right place that counts. And now, if you've done palaverin', mebbe you'll leave me to get packed up.'

Ormond laid down his empty mug, and came forward to collect his guns. As he stooped, so Hanney drew his left-hand gun, with smooth speed spun it, caught the barrel and smashed the butt down on the ramrod's head, sending him pitching to the ground.

77

The bounty-hunter continued packing his gear, then kicking the fire out, he climbed astride his pure-black Morgan gelding and rode away without another glance at the prostrate man.

Hank Ormond came to slowly, and after a time he drew himself onto his knees and rubbed his head gently. It was tender to the touch, and he cursed Hanney loud and long until the pain settled into a throbbing, dull ache. By the time he was back in the saddle his good humour was restored. He reckoned that for all Hanney had said or inferred to the contrary, the bounty-hunter wouldn't be giving Machin second chances.

Luke Withers tied the Appaloosa to the hitchrail in front of the Lazy Y and climbed the steps to the verandah carefully. He knocked on the door, and waited a long time without hearing any sound of movement. When he knocked again he heard sounds from upstairs, and at length Sally Machin's voice called out. 'Who is it?'

'It's Luke Withers, Sally,' he replied, and he heard her quick intake of breath as she released the bolt and edged the door open.

Sally's tousled head peeked round the door, then she stood back to let him in. When he came inside she moved around and stood the other side of the table, pulling her dressing-gown closer around her.

'Howdy, Luke,' she said. 'You'll have to excuse the way I look. I just tumbled out of bed after a couple of hours sleep.'

Luke took off his Stetson and twisted it around in his hand as he smiled at the girl. 'I guess you'll allus look the same to me, Sally. Anyway, I guess with the things you've got on yore mind sleep doesn't come easy, so I'm sorry I disturbed you.'

She came around the table and took the Stetson from his nervous fingers. 'I'm sure glad you did, Luke. It's good to see a friendly face for a change.' She paused while she collected a bottle and glasses. 'It's a long time since you last called, Luke, an' we've missed you.'

Withers poured a full glass for himself and just a drop for the girl; then he gave Sally a long, serious look, while she studied him and decided he really was the most handsome man she had known.

'I've missed calling, Sally, but you know how it is. I never seem to be able to get away from the livery, especially now that Pa's got the Appaloosa bug. He's set on breedin' 'em in a big way. I reckon he'd sleep with 'em if I'd let him.'

She nodded, but her face clouded as his real reason struck her. He had kept away since the accident to his leg, and she had been deeply hurt that he had made his mind up that she would feel different about him on account of his limp, and his inability to fork a cayuse for anything more than a short ride. He had forced her to seek company elsewhere.

'Who's looking after things today?' she asked.

'Seth Paget.' He was still looking at her as he spoke, and Sally felt the colour mount her cheeks. 'Seth's going east soon to learn banking, so maybe I should take on some help, so's I get some time to myself on a regular basis.'

'Yes Luke,' Sally found herself nodding almost enthusiastic agreement. 'I'd like that.' Then, modifying the statement, 'Doug an' me would be real pleased to see you more often.'

Luke reached over and took her hand in his, and the touch sent the blood coursing in both of them. 'Now Sally, what about Doug? Tell me what's happening.'

Sally started from the beginning, and went on to tell him everything she remembered up to Doug's departure and the subsequent movement of Marshal Travis. Without realizing, she had reached with her other hand and now held Luke's hand clasped tightly, drawing comfort from his strength and presence.

They were positioned so when Hank Ormond burst in. Sally released her grasp, and Luke withdrew his hand slowly and turned to welcome the ramrod. Ormond's eyes were like chips of ice; then he forced a smile to his lips.

'Hiya, Luke. You don't get to ridin' much these days. I ain't seen that rig before an' I wasn't sure who was callin', wa'al that is 'til I saw the dust marks of that foot you drag.'

Sally Machin caught her breath at Ormond's cruelty, and in that moment any regard she had ever held for the Lazy Y ramrod evaporated. Luke Withers remained unmoved. He had come to terms with his disability.

'This is the first time out for the rig, Hank,' he said quietly. 'Pa built it, an' he sure enough made a good job of it. I guess you'll soon get used to seein' it around. I aim to visit a lot more from now on.'

Ormond nodded, then turned his attention to Sally. 'I did like Doug and Travis wanted, an' Hanney's moved on.' He paused to let the fear rise in the girl. 'I'll now be doin' what you said. I'm gettin' some shut-eye like the hands 'til mid-day, then I'll be takin' 'em to collect the beeves in.'

'Thank you, Hank,' she said. 'I guess there's nothing we can do except let things take their own course.'

'It's not what I'd be doin' if it was left to me,' he replied. 'I'd nail Hanney for sure.' Then with a curt nod to Luke Withers, he stalked out of the ranch-house, and led his

81

mount into the stables, stripped the gear off and quickly settled the animal in with a feed before getting to his quarters alongside the bunkhouse.

SIX

When Luke Withers left the Lazy Y, Ormond's smouldering eyes watched him until the rig disappeared around a belt of timber. The ramrod made his mind up: Withers would have to die. There was no way he was going to allow Withers to come back into the reckoning with Sally Machin now. It had seemed that events and time were in his favour, but Withers could very easily win by persistent attendance and Sally's natural charity. Ormond knew that women discounted things like game legs when they looked for a man to settle with, and although he couldn't understand their reasoning, he wasn't prepared to leave his chances to fate. He wanted Sally Machin, and through her, the Lazy Y.

He took down the light gentling saddle from a wall-hook, and picked up his Winchester rifle before leaving his quarters by the back door. Picking his way to the furthest corral, keeping buildings between him and the ranch-house, he caught one of the cavvy cayuses and, after saddling up, rode away rapidly. At no time could he be seen from the ranch, and soon he was riding the rugged twisting trail that cut the distance to Springfield by a third. The trail joined up with the regular route down through a long, steep gully strewn with large boulders.

With plenty of time to spare, Ormond was in position, his cayuse hidden behind a boulder backtrail. His area of vision was limited, but it didn't bother him; a split second would be enough. A quarter of an hour later he heard the sound of the rig, and he settled and took aim. No more than half a minute passed and the Appaloosa preceded the rig in line with his sight, then the rig and Luke Withers, leaning forward.

Ormond felt elation flood him even as he pressed the trigger. The bark of the Winchester coincided with Withers slumping forward, and the rig passed from sight. The ramrod strained his ears to pick up the sound of continued movement, then he picked his way backtrail to collect his mount, satisfied that the Appaloosa was set to take the rig all the way to Springfield. He arrived back at his quarters unseen, and cleaned the barrel of the Winchester before lying on his bunk to while away the time until mid-day.

Joe Wallace turned into the Panhandle saloon and after ordering a beer at the bar, took a table giving him a view of everything. Half-a-dozen tables were already occupied, either by cronies talking business or inveterate drinkers dragging out a late liquid breakfast. He was half-way into his beer when Jake Caswall pushed through the swing doors and marched up to the bar. He stopped in full flight at the sight of the marshal. His lips curled in a sneer.

'Thought you'd have ridden into the sun by now, Marshal,' he growled. 'You ain't doin' any good here. Hanney'll not fail. He'll have Machin tied down across his cayuse in the next few days.'

'If Hanney kills Machin it won't mean that we'll move on.' Joe spoke slowly to let his words sink in. 'We'll still be looking for the real killer, an' when we come up with that answer, you'll stand alongside the killer for Machin's death.'

Jake Caswall stared pop-eyed at Wallace, and for a moment it seemed that he'd go for his guns. He struggled for composure, then hooted: 'You're plain loco! It had to be Machin who did the killin'. You know durned well that Machin arrived to see the old man when the others lit out for the brush, an' when Sam got in from town he found the old man dead. It couldn't be anyone 'cept Machin.'

The sheriff's half move for his guns centred Joe's attention on them. They were Navy Colts, with gold medallions inlaid into the grips. He remembered the guns fired .36 calibre slugs, and he felt a moment's elation

85

as he realized that proof of Jake Caswall's participation in the crime could be proved or disproved easily.

'We've asked our questions, Caswall, an' we're plumb sure that Machin couldn't have done the killing. It was a long time between his leavin' an' yore brother Sam arriving from town.' Joe paused and stared hard at the glowering sheriff. 'Time enough for any rider to look in an' get clear. It could've been anybody. Even you!'

Caswall's eyes closed to pinpricks, and his face went turkey-red. 'An' why in heck should I want to salivate my father?' he blurted.

'Because he hadn't paid you any dinero for six months for one thing. An' fer the roll of notes you kept showin' to thet blonde, an' the rest that went with it.'

Jake Caswall pulled himself together with an effort. 'I don't have to take account of what you think, Wallace. It don't matter a hill of beans. In my book it was Machin who did the killin', an' I set Hanney onto him fer the reasons I gave you the first time we met. As for sayin' I killed my father, if you'd said that in front of witnesses I'd have put a coupla slugs in yore hide.'

Joe shrugged the remark away. 'Anyways, I'm not bothered about Machin. There's no way Hanney'll get to him. He's bein' tailed by the slickest hombre that ever wore a US marshal's badge. I'll be makin' up my mind 'bout you in a couple of days.'

Sheriff Caswall turned abruptly and stalked to the bar. The barkeep had a bottle and glass ready and the sheriff snatched them up and took a table directly opposite Wallace, and after swilling the first glassful down he refilled the glass, to stare with basilisk ferocity at the marshal. Joe returned the look with a benign, bland expression.

Finishing his beer, Joe was contemplating a turn around town when the doors swung and Frank Caswall preceded his brothers Sam and Clem into the saloon. They saw Jake immediately, and although there was no show of pleasure on the part of the sheriff or the newcomers, they pulled out chairs and sat with him. Frank signalled to the barkeep, who brought over bottles and glasses. When the barkeep returned behind the bar, Jake Caswall leaned forward and spoke in low tones to his brothers. From the glances of Frank and Clem, who sat side-face to Wallace, he deduced that Jake was giving them an edited version of his conversation with the marshal.

When Jake sat back and concentrated his attention on his glass, the other brothers conferred for a while; then they stood up, and Frank led the way to spread out at Joe's table.

'Jake's been tellin' us how Travis is trailin' Hanney to wet-nurse Machin. Well, we reckon he oughta either let Hanney loose or press on an' bring Machin in pronto to stand trial.' Frank paused and looked to his brothers, who nodded. 'We feel it's time we took a hand, an' set after Machin.'

Joe's eyes had ranged the side-arms carried by the brothers as Frank was talking, and he saw they all toted the regular Colt .45. When he switched his gaze to Frank his eyes were like chips of ice.

'When you hombres have finished yore business in town, you'd best get back to yore own graze an' stay there.' Sam's expression remained calm, but Frank and Clem were suddenly deadpan; the look that went with itchy fingers. Joe continued quickly: 'Just think afore you fly off the handle. You've been quick to pick on Machin as the killer, but it could as well have been any of you brothers.' Joe held his hand up to stem their angry replies. 'You an' Clem saw Machin afore you left,' he said to Frank. 'We've just got yore word that neither of you came back.' He switched to Sam. 'We've only got your word that yore father was killed afore you arrived back from town. You could have killed him, muffling the noise with cloth before callin' in Daley an' Smart. An' again, the sheriff might have bin ridin' early, watched you an' Machin ride away, an' did the killin' himself. Now I'm not sayin' that any of you are guilty, but when you talk of trackin' down Machin I get to thinkin' that a dead, innocent Machin would let the real killer off the hook. So, I'll make it plain. You hombres head out after Machin, an' I'll be gunnin' for you.'

'You wouldn't get much luck, Marshal!' Clem Caswall snarled. 'You'd end up on a shutter takin' the Caswalls on.'

Joe shrugged. 'It don't need to come to any showdown. I'm bankin' on you hombres havin' the good sense to leave things to the men paid fer doin' the job.' The turned his attention to his beer, while the Caswall brothers stood irresolute for a minute, then Frank nodded to the other two.

'C'mon,' he said. 'Let's get a few drinks under our belts. I reckon the marshal's put it on the line plumb right.'

They returned to their table, and passed on the details of the conversation to Jake. Joe, watching closely, saw the sheriff's face become almost apoplectic with rage. Then, after a while, the man's choler subsided and he fortified himself with a couple more glasses of spirit; his eyes held a hunted look.

The marshal sauntered to the door, debating what to do next. Then, making his decision to get everything down on paper, he walked around to the hotel entrance and went to his room. He added the conversations and his observations to his and Travis' records, and studied the result for a long time; then, intending to put one question to the test, he set off for the funeral parlour.

Wes Slade was sitting in the front office, a glass in his hand and his feet up on the table. He was a cheery-looking, rosy-faced man, as bald as a coot, in no way resembling the usual run of morticians Joe had known.

Slade took in the badge and nodded affably. 'Howdy, Marshal. Get yoreself parked in a chair.' He pushed a bottle and a glass across the table. 'Help yoreself, an' when you've oiled yore throat tell me what I can do for you. Er – the moniker's Wes Slade, that's if you didn't read the shingle.'

Joe grinned widely. 'Howdy Wes, they call me Joe Wallace.'

The marshal took time to pour himself a glass, and take a tentative sip, then put his question bluntly: 'Just who've I got to see in this hyar burg, Wes, to get one of yore clients dug up?'

Slade's boots came down to earth, and he sat upright to stare at Joe. 'Gawd,' he breathed. 'Now why in heck would you want to do that?'

'Evidence,' Joe replied enigmatically. 'I guess I'm at the cross-roads, an' if I took a peek at a hombre in Boot Hill, I'd get a better notion which trail to take.'

'Which hombre? An' what're you lookin' fer?'

'Dave Caswall, an' I'd like to know what calibre slug killed him.'

Wes Slade's breath exhaled in a relieved sigh, and his boots came back onto the table. He took a gulp at his glass, then smiled at Wallace contentedly. 'You sure enough had me worried, Joe,' he said. 'Once is enough to bury anyone, but this time there ain't no need to do it twice. No sirree. An' you don't have to ask anyone's permission to get the evidence you want. When you've finished yore drink I'll take you through an' show you.'

'How come you've got the evidence?' Joe asked, mystified.

'When I got to tidying Dave up, the hole in him was big 'nough to put yore fist through, an' the second slug went deeper, exposing the first. Anyway, it showed plain as plain, so I dug it out, an' put it in a little box with a note. It's not the first I've dug out by a long way, that's why I put a note in with 'em. My helper, Cy Charis, was alongside o' me at the time.'

Joe drained his drink and they went through to the workroom together. Cy Charis was measuring timbers and only spared a glance for them. Wes Slade went to a cabinet with glass doors and opening up he reached in for the last box in a long row. He handed it to Joe without a word. The box was no more than two inches square, and Joe opened the tiny brass hasp, taking out the slug and the note. The note merely stated the date of death, date of interment and Dave Caswall's name. The slug eliminated Sheriff Caswall from consideration as the killer. It was a .45.

'Wa'al, I'm sure obliged to you, Wes. Just one thing; keep this under yore hat.' And when Slade nodded, 'What made you keep all these slugs?'

Slade smiled. 'I guess it's a deadly job, so I pick on anything to liven up interest in it.'

Joe took his leave of the mortician and treated himself to a meal at the eating-house as an aid to sorting out his thoughts. When he finally cleared his plate and disposed of the last dregs of coffee he came to the rueful conclusion that he was left with his instincts. It seemed he had merely contrived to clear the Caswall brothers of complicity, leaving Doug Machin still out on a limb. He only had Doug's word, given to Travis, that Dave Caswall was on the verandah when he left. Without conscious thought he headed towards the livery and collected his cayuse from Seth Paget.

'If you're headin' for the Lazy Y,' Seth said, as Joe climbed astride his sturdy mustang, 'an meet Luke, just tell him he's got no call to hurry. I've got things in hand.'

'I'll tell him,' Joe called over his shoulder as he rode towards the north trail. When the trail allowed, he let his mount stretch its gait in the hope that the wind of his passage would clear the fog from his mind. His circle of thought came to an abrupt stop when, after half-an-hour, he rounded a bend at the entrance to a canyon to come upon Luke Withers' rig. Luke was dabbing at the side of his head with a blood-spattered handkerchief, and the Appaloosa's flanks were heaving.

The marshal came alongside the rig, and for a few moments Withers looked at him without any show of recognition; then slowly awareness came into his eyes.

'What happened?' Joe asked.

Luke shook his head, then grimaced with pain at the movement. 'I dunno – I'd just come up to Henshaw Pass when I saw a rattler on the left-hand side. I guess I turned my head to look at it when I heard a shot an' passed out. I reckon that rattler saved my life. I must have come to just after the Appaloosa stopped, judgin' by the way he's still blowing.'

Joe dismounted and rounded the rig to take a look at Luke's head. There was a groove an inch and a half long where the hair had been sliced away and blood was suppurating along the length of the wound. 'Yeah,' Joe agreed, 'you sure owe that rattler a favour, Luke. You gonna be all right now to drive home?'

'I reckon so,' he replied.

'I'll mosey along an' see if I can pick up any sign. How far away is Henshaw Pass?'

Luke Withers looked around the canyon walls to orientate himself, before replying: 'About twelve miles. It's a quick route to the Lazy Y, but it's rough goin'.'

'Who was at the Lazy Y when you left?' Joe asked.

Luke thought about it before saying, 'Wa'al, Sally was in the house, the hands were asleep after spendin' the best of the night lookin' out for Hanney, an' Ormond had been in his quarters half-an-hour after leavin' Sally an' me. Doug Machin left last night to get clear of Hanney, an' Marshal Travis is tailin' Hanney.'

'Any of the Lazy Y hands got any reason for salivating you?'

'No, none of the hands,' Luke replied. 'Ormond's never been a close buddy on account that Sally an' me are friendly, but I guess he's getting some shut-eye, he's been on the go all night.'

'One thing I know for sure,' Joe told him, 'it wasn't any of the Caswall brothers who dry-gulched you. I left 'em in town after having had 'em in sight for long enough.' As he spoke the Marshal climbed back into the saddle, and waited while Luke Withers took up the reins and set the Appaloosa off at a steady pace.

It was an hour later when the marshal turned his mustang into the gully that Withers had called Henshaw Pass. He had noted where the Appaloosa had been startled into a rapid gait – the slip marks caused by the animal's hind hoofs as it dug in for impetus showed up – and having decided where Withers would have been in relation to the horse, lined up the likely place the marksman would have lain. It was alongside a massive boulder that dwarfed and sheltered a smaller one beside it, and, surely enough, part of the surface of the smaller boulder had been wiped clear of dust to remove the imprint of the would-be assassin's body. He was able to pick out a few footprints going to and from the boulder to where a cayuse had stood backtrail.

Henshaw Pass proved to be a tough, rugged route to the Lazy Y graze; for most of the way there was insufficient room for two riders to pass, and the mustang was scrambling and climbing over slippery or loose surfaces all the way. It was as well that the mustang, true to its breed, was as sure-footed as a bighorn sheep, and Joe heaved a sigh of relief when the Pass gave way to rolling grassland.

It didn't take the marshal long to pick up the signs which led him eventually to a point in the remuda corral furthest from and out of sight of the Lazy Y ranch-house, where a post could be lifted out of the ground and pulled away, bringing the barbed wire strands with it, leaving space for animals to pass through. There were only a few cayuses in the corral, and to his practised eye none of them showed signs of having been hard-ridden recently.

There was no way Joe could pick up signs in the corral. It was clear to him that the hands had recently collected their mounts for working cattle out of the brush, so he rode around to take a look at the bunk-house. The place was empty, so he continued to the ranch-house, where he tied his mustang to the hitchrail and, climbing the steps, knocked on the door.

Sally Machin opened up and eyed him uncertainly.

'Sorry to worry you, Ma'am, but I'd like to ask you a few questions.'

She opened the door wide. 'Come on in, Marshal, and take a seat. I've just made some coffee if you'd like some, or would you prefer bourbon?'

'Coffee will do just fine, Ma'am,' he replied, as he took a seat at the table.

The girl brought in a tray and poured two mugs, passing one to the marshal. She waited for him to sip at the scalding coffee, then sat back, waiting for the young lawman to ask his questions.

'Wa'al, Ma'am, did you see Doug away on the morning he went to visit Dave Caswall?'

'Yes, like always. He likes me to get his breakfast, no matter what time.'

'Was there anyone else around at that time?'

'Yeah, Curly Waters the cook, and Hank Ormond. Hank wanted to visit a couple of lineshacks, and knowing Doug was leaving early for the Flying Diamond he'd told Waters to be around for an early breakfast, so that he could ride part of the way with Doug. They rode off together.'

'An' this morning, Luke Withers called, that right?' Sally nodded.

'Tell me, who else was around when he was here?'

The girl looked at him sharply. 'Why?' she asked.

'Because somebody dry-gulched him when he was crossing the mouth of Henshaw Pass.' He stopped when he saw the look of alarm spring to Sally's eyes. 'He's all right,' he hastened to add, 'the slug just creased his scalp an' knocked him out fer a bit. I watched him drive away to Springfield.'

She breathed a sigh of relief. 'There was no-one else; the hands were all asleep, they'd been out in the night keeping Hanney boxed in. Ormond came in, but he left to get some sleep about half-an-hour before Luke left. They've all gone now to bring in the mavericks out of the brush with the rest onto the home graze, ready for the drive.'

'So, when Withers left you were the only one around.'

'Yeah, that's so. And as soon as he rounded that copse I went back to bed. I'd been up most of the night.'

Joe drained his coffee, then stood up. 'Wa'al, thank you Ma'am, I reckon that answers all my questions.' He made his way to the door, then swung around and looked squarely at the girl. 'Just how do you figure Ormond? Is he something special to you?'

Sally Machin stared at him, her expression changing. 'I guess he's a friend as well as the ramrod,' she replied slowly. 'He was no more than fifteen when my father took him on, and he was that good when Luke Smith, the old ramrod, went east to be offered the job by my father, an' he's done a good job ever since.'

'No more special than friend?' Joe persisted.

Two pink spots appeared high on Sally's cheeks. 'I don't know you've got any right to ask, Marshal Wallace, but no, he's no more than a friend to me.' It seemed for a moment that she had said her piece, then she blurted out: 'If he thinks any different, I've not given him the cause.'

'Thank you, Ma'am,' Joe said, his face spread with his beguiling smile. 'Some questions I don't like asking, but believe me, I had to know.'

He left Sally Machin staring after him, and thinking that with his charm he'd wheedle answers out of any woman.

SEVEN

Later in the day Jake Caswall came out of
the Panhandle saloon clutching a couple of
bottles to replenish the private supply in his
office, still seething with a desire to termin-
ate Marshal Wallace's existence. He wanted
sleeping dogs left to lie, and Machin dead,
then he'd get his proper share of the Flying
Diamond. In addition, his brother Clem
would be alienated from Sally Machin, and
she'd be fair game for his own type of ap-
proach, being out on a limb. He had toyed
with dry-gulching the marshal himself, but
reason prevailed, and his fertile mind played
around the problem endlessly. The answer
came as his hot eyes lit upon the two men
emerging from Bodin's hotel.

'Howdy, Sheriff,' Mick Shield said, as he
and his pardner, Ferdy Ballard, drew level.
Ballard nodded affably.

'I'd like to palaver with you jaspers,' Caswall barked. 'Mebbe you'll look in soon.'

The two men looked at each other, then
Ballard shrugged and gave Caswall a hard
look. 'If it's something we can do before the
night-stage tomorrow, then that's all right,'
he said, 'but we're takin' that coach for sure.

We're headin' for Clayton, New Mexico. The place'll be bustin' to the seams fer a week with the rodeo bein' there, an' we aim to get among the big spenders.'

'There's nothing to stop you catchin' thet coach,' Jake Caswall said. 'Get it booked if you want, then call in at the gaolhouse.'

An hour or so and a bottle later, Shield and Ballard left Jake Caswall with a satisfied smile on his face. They could be trusted to engineer the situation that would end with the elimination of Deputy Marshal Joe Wallace. Both men were deadly gun-slingers, and he would be able to clear them on a claim of self-defence, leaving Marshal Travis high and dry when he returned. There was no way Travis would be able to tie the two gamblers in with anything relating to the death of Dave Caswall, or the Machins. He'd just have to accept that his pardner died on account of prodding folk too far.

Doug Machin was in his element. The night was pitch black, and every inch of the terrain he traversed was clear in his mind. Naturally observant, he also had a photographic memory, together with instant recall. As Travis had previously told him, he would have been worth a fortune to the railway companies now starting to snake inland from both east and west coasts. But his concern now was to leave a trail for Hanney that would make him dizzy.

By daylight he had half circled the first craggy hill before crossing over it through a mountain pass and taking a thin, precarious Bighorn sheep-trail around it almost to the first cross-over point; then on the next crossing he had travelled the bed of a trickling stream which crossed the regular trail to join the larger stream which crossed both the Lazy Y and Flying Diamond spreads, before emptying into the Cimarron River. Here he had picked his route along the banks amongst the trees, his eyes perfectly attuned to the dark. Before leaving the bulk of the hill he had crossed the stream and, gaining the top of the bank, had set off across the rolling grassland to the next hill, where, under safe cover and a good view of the hill where he had laid the false trails, he ate a good breakfast and gave the animals a breather.

The young rancher grinned to himself as he reached into his food package for more. Hanney would be under way by now, confident in his ability to get his chore done quickly and easily. He sure had one heck of a disappointment due. He was going to be all saddle-sore and riled something awful before he hit the clear trail to Las Animas. Mebbe he shouldn't have given Travis the plan of his intended route. It was still Travis' intention to take him in for trial, and anything could happen in a trial, so perhaps the lawman should have been made to work for his success. Doug sobered at the thought, and in his new mood wondered who could have killed Dave Caswall. The Caswall brothers he discounted; Dave hadn't pressured them since they'd grown up. Dave had known that Sam, Frank and Clem could be depended upon to look after things and still do the work of two normal hands, and he had never worried about them causing the odd ruckus in town. He had reckoned town was for hell-raising, anyhow. When Doug thought of Jake however, doubts crowded in, and the more he thought about the sheriff and the frosty eyes with which Dave Caswall had observed him the last couple of times he had seen the two together, made him conclude that Jake would have been capable, given the opportunity that morning, and taken it, then not wasted a second before setting Hanney on the trail.

The early morning mist rolled up the hills from the stream, enveloping him briefly before rising skyward. After studying the intervening country to the hill where he had spent the hours of darkness, and seeing no movement, he remounted and made his way off the trail and through a gully to a shallow blind valley where grass grew. Here he stripped the gear from the cayuses and turned them free to graze, before stretching his length and smoking a couple of cigarettes.

When the animals were satisfied, Doug draped the gear around them, changing their duties to even the effort before returning to the trail. This time he made a straight passage, and, reaching the plain, headed north-west, keeping the bulk of the hill to hide him from anyone on the first hill armed with a spy-glass. It was mid-day before he entered the rugged bulk of foothills, backed by mountains, where he intended to make life difficult for Hanney. For the rest of the day, after clearing the foothill, he created a trail that would sorely test the bounty-hunter. When darkness fell he had made his descent, and was headed east across a wide expanse of prairie that sloped imperceptibly downwards. At daybreak he was heading north-north-east in the general direction of Las Animas.

Moss Hanney rode down close to the Lazy Y headquarters before stopping to fit muffles to the Morgan's hooves. He knew he had a clear hour before Ormond would be sufficiently recovered to find his way back, and the hands would have hit their bunks the moment they rode in. He toyed with the idea of taking some of the starch out of Machin's sister, but shelved the pleasant thought because although Ormond had stated that Travis had opted out, he was never prepared to take anyone's word at face value.

As he rode in, silently as a wraith, between

the ranch-house and stables, he had plumbed the reasoning behind Ormond's words and actions. The ramrod's purpose was clear to him. Ormond wanted Machin dead. All the talk had been for the purpose of urging him not to waste time on a cat and mouse stalk, but to salivate the rancher the first moment a chance came up.

Just a glance inside the stable gave him enough evidence that Machin had gone, and his sharp eyes picked up signs that a ridden horse and packhorse had headed towards the nearest hill. The man's over-active sixth sense told him that equally sharp eyes were watching him, but he paid no attention. He felt sure the watcher was Marshal Travis. With a bitter smile, the bounty-hunter climbed back into the saddle and rode away in the general direction of the hill.

When clear of the Lazy Y headquarters, he removed the muffles and rode slowly until the sun was up. Coming to a fold in the rolling grassland he dismounted, leaving the Morgan gelding to graze while he stretched his length and stared at the hill through his telescope. For a long time he ranged the telescope along the entire hill, making out every ravine and gully. He saw where three separate streams ran from springs and joined the tributary that ran across the foot of the hill, before winding away in the distance north-west towards the western side of the next hill.

When Hanney finally got back into the saddle he had the picture clear in mind, and, unerringly, he changed direction towards the trail that Machin had taken to first climb from the plain. Gaining the trail, he allowed himself an evil grin of satisfaction as he immediately picked up sign of a ridden and led horse. Having climbed sufficiently high, he halted long enough to quarter the terrain to the Lazy Y headquarters, but of Marshal Travis there was no sign.

He followed the trail around the lower slopes of the hill, to where Machin had taken the high pass from the east side to the west, and joined the higher and more hazardous trail that led across the breast to where the other hill came into view. Hanney snorted with temper as the sign showed that Machin had again travelled round the east side, and he concluded that in this particular, Ormond had spoken nothing but the truth. Machin sure did leave a trail that made a hombre dizzy. Savagely, Hanney admitted to himself that he'd have to put his thinking cap on. Machin must have laid this trail in darkness; given daylight the rancher would have him running in tight circles, and that was a strange and new experience that filled Hanney with dark hate.

Eventually, the bounty-hunter shrugged the problem away, settling for his experience of the chase to eventually get him in the right position. He also felt that he had now got inside Machin's mind; he reckoned on the young rancher, having created a maze on this the first hill, and maybe by now the next, making a fast break to give himself a good lead. So, without further preamble, he rode to plain level and headed for the next hill. Halfway between he again picked up Machin's trail, which he followed without difficulty. He saw the tracks both in and out of the gully which led to the blind valley, and continued right across the face of the hill down to the plain and on to the next, then into the mountainous bulk beyond.

Two days later a bemused, totally frustrated and angry bounty-hunter broke free of the mountain mass and set his Morgan in the straightest line for Las Animas. A few times that day his skin had crawled with the certain knowledge that somewhere a rifle was trained on him. It was a totally new experience for Hanney, and even in the cold mountain air the perspiration had pumped out of his pores. It would have made him happier to have known that even though his instinct was serving him well, the man at the business end of the rifle had been Marshal Travis. Hanney was building up a reputation in his mind for Machin that placed the $1,000 dead-or-alive tag in different perspective.

As he held his course away from where he believed Machin to be, he determined to telegraph Sheriff Caswall to up the ante. Caswall had made the young rancher out to be a push-over, but Hanney now knew the sheriff lied. He suspected that it suited the sheriff, equally as much as Ormond, to have Machin dead. Well, they'd have to pay through the nose.

Deputy Marshal Wallace slid out of the saddle outside the livery with a sigh of satisfaction. He was within a stone's-throw of a good meal, and his mind was busily playing around with the choices when young Seth Paget came out to take over his bay mustang.

'Howdy, Seth,' Joe said, 'how's Luke now?'

The youngster gave him a broad smile. 'He's as good as a new pin,' he replied. 'The doc took a look at him an' patched him up. He's inside anyway, checking through his stocks, then he's gonna get some chow.'

'I'll guess I'll join him then,' Joe said as Seth led the mustang inside. He found Luke Withers in the grain store, pencilling notes into a ledger.

'How's it feelin' now?' he asked, as Luke turned to greet him.

'No more'n a bit sore,' Luke replied. 'The doc said there was nothing spoiled, but that I'd sure been lucky. Considerin' all, I'll never throw promiscuous lead at a rattler again.'

Joe laughed with him before saying, 'Seth told me you're gonna grab some chow; if you're good an' ready I'll keep you company.'

Luke nodded and led the way to the office, where he threw the ledger on the desk before grabbing his Stetson. Then, calling out to tell Seth he was going, he preceded the marshal outside, and together they made their way to the eating-house.

As they relaxed with mugs of coffee while their meal was being prepared, Joe referred to his recent conversation with Sally Machin, and in particular to his questions concerning Hank Ormond. Luke's eyes shone like stars when Joe related the girl's answers, and the thoughts that ran on from the acquired knowledge sent him into a reverie of introspection so that he hardly heard Joe's following remarks. He came out of his brown study and looked apologetically at the marshal.

'Huh, I guess I didn't hear what you said then, Joe. I reckon I was too busy buildin' up my own pictures of what Miss Sally was thinking deep down.' He looked shamefaced. 'What was it you said?'

Joe grinned. 'What I said was that Hank Ormond rode alongside Doug Machin on that morning before sun-up. They were due to part company so that Machin would go to the Flying Diamond, and Ormond to check up on a couple of lineshacks. Doug not having said anything to the contrary, it seems that's what they did.' The marshal paused, and now his face was serious. 'So it wasn't only Doug Machin out ridin' that morning. I just wonder where they parted company. It gets me to wondering who else was riding the range.'

Luke poured out a couple more mugs of coffee as he mulled over the point, then he looked up sharply as something came to mind. 'Most anybody could've left on the south trail an' circled the town to hit the Flying Diamond, so there's no way of bein' certain, but one hombre passed the livery that morning in plenty of time to be at the Flying Diamond by sun-up, an' that's Jake Caswall. The cayuse he forks allus steps light on his right foreleg. There ain't nothin' wrong with the crittur, it's just the way he's made, I guess; but there's no way I wouldn't recognize thet cayuse.' Luke paused, with Joe deep in thought, then he continued: 'Mind, in fairness, there ain't nothing special in the sheriff ridin' at that time of night. He gets most of his ridin' at that time of night. He gets most of his ridin' done between a couple of hours before sun-up to mid-morning. He mostly spends the day around town.'

Lin San came up with their meals at that point, and Joe gave himself up wholeheartedly to the pleasure of eating. Luke Withers couldn't help but notice Joe's total absorption and enjoyment, but he gave up trying to match Joe's speed of mastication, and he was only halfway through his meal before Lin San was alongside, taking Joe's repeat order.

When the Chinaman had departed, Joe leaned across to catch Luke's eye. 'Thet Jake Caswall,' he said, 'did you ever see him tote anything other than those Navy Colts?'

'You mean the fancy ones with the gold medallions on the handles?' And when Joe nodded, Luke shook his head. 'Nope. They belonged to Billy Shanklin, the hombre Ormond salivated three years ago. I guess Caswall fancied 'em an' figgered he might as well wear 'em as leave 'em in a drawer in his office. I've never seen him without 'em since.' His curiosity got the better of him. 'Does it mean anything special to you?'

'Yeah,' Joe answered drily. 'It's just made positive something I felt was doubtful. Anyway, you've given me some more to think about.'

Luke didn't pry any further; he realized that a lawman was in no position to spread his thoughts around. A US marshal needed to keep things close to his chest if he wanted to keep a whole skin while he dug for the answers to any unwitnessed crime.

When they had paid Lin San, Joe suggested they had a beer in the Panhandle saloon and Luke agreed readily. He had developed a liking for the big, ungainly marshal, and felt comfortable in his company.

They had scarcely settled down to their table when Jake Caswall, who had been sitting in his customary place, got up and walked out into the street without giving them a glance. There was a good-sized crowd in the saloon for the time of day, and several girls from the dance-hall opposite were mingling with the eager customers. Some of the girls flashed quick glances at the two men, but neither showed interest and the girls looked for other, easier victims.

Another girl came through the swing doors, closely followed by two men in gamblers' garb, and she made all the others look tawdry by comparison. Her dress of sheer silk drew every eye, and the low-cut cleavage showed her generous, milk-white breasts to full advantage, so that most eyes remained on her. When she sat down between the two gamblers, there was a lot of shifting around by customers at other tables to keep her in sight.

Joe grinned across at Luke Withers. 'She's sure popular,' he said.

'Huh!' Luke exclaimed. 'She looks good 'nough to eat, but believe me, Rhoda Cluney's pure poison. Spends a lot of time with those hombres, Shields an' Ballard.'

The marshal gave the gamblers a quick look and found them weighing him with cool, shrewd eyes. They looked away, disinterest ostentatiously displayed. Shields called the barkeep, who sent over an oldster carrying bottles and glasses on a tray. Ballard poured out drinks, giving the girl a full glass. She drank the fiery liquid without taking the glass from her lips, and Ballard refilled it with a grin.

Joe finished his beer, catching up with Withers who stood up to take the glasses for refills. 'I'll get 'em, Luke,' the marshal said, but remembering Withers' game leg, and the man's independence, he settled back in his seat and rolled himself a cigarette. He lit up and contemplated the gamblers and the sultry Rhoda Cluney.

With deft fingers the girl was building a cigarette. She inspected it, appearing satisfied, then she spoke to the two men, who shook their heads; then, glancing at Joe's burning cigarette, she crossed to his table, and leaning over close to him she asked for a light. When Joe reached for matches she came even closer; then to his amazement she backed away from him, screaming abuse and accusations of ungentlemanly handling. Mike Shield and Ballard were on their feet, their expressions hostile.

'You no-good maverick!' shouted Shields. 'You ain't gonna hide behind that badge! Reach!'

At the bar, Luke, in the act of turning with the brimming glasses, was amazed to see the girl leaping away from Wallace, mouthing accusations, and when Shield shouted his threatening words he saw that Ballard was already holding a gun pointed at Wallace, but masked by the Stetson on the table.

Shields went for his gun as tables behind him, in line with Wallace, went crashing as men and women flung themselves to safety. The glasses Luke Withers held went crashing to the floor as he clawed for his gun.

For all his ungainly size Marshal Wallace moved with incredible speed. He slid out of the chair to his left, his right-hand gun already in hand, balling his legs and rolling beneath the tables. Two bullets from Shields' gun thudded into the floor boards, a split second before Joe fired, and the gambler pitched across the table with a hole in his forehead. At the same moment Ballard let out an almighty yell as the bullet from Luke Withers' gun smashed through his wrist. Rhoda Cluney screamed and pranced back in horror.

While Joe regained his feet and brushed himself down, Luke Withers stepped away from the bar and crossed to the girl. His eyes bored into her, and he pointed the gun at her head. 'You've got one chance, an' one chance only. An' make it loud an' clear. Tell everybody it was a put-up job, an' the marshal did no more than light yore cigarette.'

For a long moment Rhoda Cluney stared into Luke's face, then looked around wildly for help. But although every eye was upon her, none gave her any hope; nobody was going to stick his neck out with the law on her account.

'Yeah! Yeah!' she yelled. 'They forced me into it! Said they'd cut my face up if I didn't do like they said! They watched you from the eating-house, an' had a gun in my back until you turned into the Panhandle.'

Even in the midst of his pain, Ferdy Ballard turned an incredulous eye on the girl, but he said nothing. If things had turned out right Rhoda would have stuck to her accusation; he could hardly blame her looking for a way out.

Luke holstered his gun, and the girl almost ran out of the saloon into the street, where she quickly calmed down to present the picture that would soon have the menfolk running and drooling over her.

A tubby oldster, who announced himself as Doc Oldfield to Joe, quickly took charge of Ferdy Ballard, and led him to the marshal's table before fixing a temporary dressing on the man's shattered wrist. He then stood aside for the marshal to question the wounded man. Luke Withers rejoined Wallace at the table after collecting two more glasses of beer. Joe smiled his thanks, then leaned towards the unfortunate Ballard, giving him a cold, baleful look.

'I've never set eyes on you two hombres

before,' he said, waving a hand in the direction of Mick Shield's corpse, which was being removed at the instruction of Wes Slade the mortician who had been attracted by the fireworks. 'An' so you had no cause to trump up the play-actin' on yore own accounts. That means you set it up fer somebody else. Who was it?'

Ballard shook his head. 'I don't know, Marshal. I thought Mick Shields had his own reasons. He allus called the ante, an' there was no way I could back out; he'd have filled me full o' lead without turnin' a hair. If I could've shook free of Shields I'd have done so long ago. Fifteen years I've had to play along with that hombre, an' I'm glad to see him get his come-uppance. I did like I was told because he was watchin' me. I had you covered behind my hat, an' could've dropped you cold before you slid from sight, but I didn't.'

Neither Wallace nor Luke Withers believed the man, but for the moment Joe chose not to pursue the matter. He nodded to Doc Oldfield: 'Mebbe you'd like to take him to your surgery an' fix him up,' he said, and when the doctor replied in the affirmative, continued: 'I'll get the sheriff to collect him an' get him locked up while I ask a few questions.'

'Leave that to me,' Doc Oldfield said. 'Ballard can stay at my place for a few days. That arm's gonna take a lot of care, an' it'll save me goin' back an' fore to that gaol-house.'

Just at that moment Jake Caswall entered the saloon, sending the batwing doors swinging furiously. His hot eyes swept around the place, settling on the doctor leading Ferdy Ballard away, then on Wallace and Withers. As Ballard followed Doc Oldfield, and came alongside the sheriff, he stared deep into the lawman's eyes, and Joe noticed the spasm of alarm flash across Caswall's face before he pulled himself together and stalked pompously to where the two men had resumed their seats and contemplated their beer.

'What was all the ruckus about?' he asked, in a loud, authoritative voice.

Joe looked up at him with a hard, frosty glance. 'I was gonna ask you the same question. I guess they've been around Springfield long enough for you to know what motivates 'em. Now me, I've never seem 'em before.'

Jake Caswall's breath exhaled in a sharp, explosive burst of temper. 'How in heck am I supposed to know what goes on in folks' mind just 'cause I happen to see 'em around most days? The only trouble those hombres got into was on account a lot of card-players don't like losing. Any killin' they've done was allus in self-defence.'

'Well, this time it wasn't, an' their luck was plumb out,' Joe replied. 'In fact it was a clever bit of actin' to get me to Boot Hill pronto. I reckon they were workin' for some-body else who needs me dead, so I'm telling you to collect Ballard from Doc Oldfield's when the doc tells you, and lock him up. I intend findin' out who he was workin' for.'

Sheriff Caswall's face mottled with temper, but once again a hunted look clouded his eyes. 'An' who's supposed to keep watch over him?' he snarled.

Joe Wallace hauled himself up to his con-siderable height and, coming close to the sheriff, he prodded a bony forefinger into the man's chest. 'You will!' he said firmly. 'You or an appointed deputy. That's if you want to stay sheriff of Springfield.'

Caswall's mouth shaped words, but no sounds came. He struggled to stifle back the choler, then turned on his heel and stamped angrily towards the doors, sending a couple of tables in his path crashing. Men watched him go in amazement, but they kept their eyes averted from the marshal and livery-man, who resumed their seats to finish off their beer. Joe smiled across at Luke Withers.

'Thanks, Luke,' he said quietly. 'I'm sure glad you had your eyes on Ballard. No matter what he said to the contrary, he was tryin' to bring that smoke-pole to bear when you got him.'

'I reckon I should've salivated him,' Luke replied feelingly. 'He was in it up to his neck, no matter what he says. There was no

117

way that Ballard lived in fear of Shields. The other way round I could understand, but they allus worked together as a team.'

Joe nodded. 'Yeah, that's what I guessed. Anyway, it looks like I'm gettin' too close to somebody for the killin' of Dave Caswall. Could be somebody who hasn't come into my reckoning yet. Who is there in Springfield who was close enough to Shield an' Ballard to make 'em either rub me out as a favour, or to put enough pressure on 'em to do the job anyway?'

'The only hombre I know who drinks with 'em regularly, an' seems to win more often than not with 'em, is Jake Caswall,' Luke answered. 'The other Caswalls have never been close to 'em, but they haven't been unfriendly either.'

Wallace considered this for a while, then stood up. 'Well, I guess I'll let things stir around in my mind for a bit, so I'll get myself some shut-eye to help things along, an' I'll leave you to get on with yore stock-taking.'

Luke Withers nodded as he hauled himself upright. 'Keep yore door locked, an' don't close more'n one eye,' he said, in half jocular manner as they parted company.

EIGHT

Carl Travis had Moss Hanney in sight practically all of the second day the bounty-hunter spent in the mountains. The plan that Doug Machin had given him showed up the devious trail that Hanney would be inveigled into taking, and also indicated a vantage point that would always overlook the route, and provide his mount with thin graze.

It was approaching late afternoon, with the sun reflecting brassily from every surface, when Hanney again came within Travis' orbit. The man was slouched in the saddle, staring at the ground, and finally he brought his cayuse to a stop beside the bed of a trickling mountain stream. He lowered himself from the saddle in a slow, cumbersome manner that spoke volumes for the man's depleted ego and low spirits.

For the next half-hour Carl Travis watched Hanney walk up and down the stream to where it disappeared overside a vertical wall of rock, to gather together about fifty feet down and to swirl along its lower bed. At length, after getting on his knees to study the opposite side of the stream from which he had approached, he must have found the trail Machin had left for him. He followed it on foot for about fifty yards, at right angles to the stream, then, when the sign pointed uphill, Hanney stared upwards for a long time, as though rooted to the spot.

Travis grinned as he glanced down at the plan. Hanney was due a lot of problems yet. Machin seemed as adept at removing sign as creating it, because the bounty-hunter was now covering old ground, just fifty yards to the south of where he had previously travelled, and the trail was due to disappear into the stream again. He watched Hanney return to his cayuse, and after taking out a package from a saddle-bag, sit on a boulder to eat. Ten minutes later the man stood up, stared across and up the face of the mountain, then held his fists high, shaking them in sheer despair. Then without further ado Hanney climbed back into the saddle, and looking neither to right nor left he set his mount to the easiest way to the plains.

The lawman whistled up Red, and quickly packing away his gear he climbed into the saddle and set about keeping Hanney in view. It wasn't difficult; the bounty-hunter was making no attempt at concealment, riding hunch-shouldered, apparently concerned only with the quickest and easiest route; and when, a couple of hours later, Hanney rode into the valley and skirted the foothill to head direct north-north-east, Travis reckoned he was making for Las Animas.

For a long time Travis nibbled away at Hanney's reasons for giving up the chase. He was not prepared to believe that the bounty-hunter could be deterred by the skilful laying of false trails. As a breed they were dogged, determined trackers, and mostly no matter how their quarry twisted and turned the bounty-hunter would get his man. It was all to do with the difference between hunting and being hunted – persistent hunting mostly ended with the prey dead; and Hanney was better than most. Perhaps the man now considered $1,000 poor reward for the chase, and intended negotiating a new and more realistic sum from his head-quarters at Las Animas. Or maybe he didn't like US marshals so close to the action. He could be planning on earning his money the easy way at a later date, when both marshals were long gone.

Carl gave the problem up at length. His concern now was to keep Hanney in sight, or well within range. Both Machin and Hanney were moving in the direction of Las Animas, and the bounty-hunter was at least half a day nearer to the rancher than Machin sus-pected. During the remaining hours of daylight Travis kept the bounty-hunter for the most part in view. Using every fold and feature of the rolling terrain, he slowly closed the distance without ever placing himself in a position to alert Hanney.

With the dying rays of the sun Hanney pulled away from the canyon that spread out in front of him, and picked a route along the face of the mountain, then just before night closed in he turned into the mountain. Travis deduced that the bounty-hunter was holing up for the night, so he selected a deep fold that would keep him and Red from Hanney's view come daylight, and after chewing his way through some hard tack, settled down under the strengthening stars.

Long before daylight the marshal had breakfasted from more hard tack and water, and had Red all saddled up ready to go. Then, with the first light of day, he saw Hanney emerge from his hole in the mountain to continue along the face. When the time was right Travis climbed into the saddle and restarted the painstaking chore of keeping the bounty-hunter under surveillance.

Daybreak found Doug Machin just thirty miles from Las Animas. He reckoned on entering the town an hour or so after midday. The terrain had altered to wildly undulating plain, with runs, arroyos, dry washes, rocky outcrops and sparse outcrops and sparse tree cover on all sides. The trail from Chinooga Springs to Las Animas was a few miles to the east, but Doug intended giving it a wide berth until much nearer Las Animas.

Now and again when riding along the face of rising ground, he pulled his mount to a halt and, gaining the ridge, quartered the backtrail with scrupulous care, but of Hanney there was no sign, and Doug felt deep satisfaction at the thought of the bounty-hunter still following a dud trail. In consequence he dismissed Hanney from his thoughts; time enough to worry about him if and when the man trailed him to the town.

He had ridden about six miles since daybreak when he saw at the bottom of a long slope a thin trail that had branched from the Chinooga Springs to Las Animas Trail and disappeared from view to the west beyond a group of redwoods. Directly ahead a gig lay on its side, and a woman was inspecting the left foreleg of a rangy-looking paint. Without hesitation Doug headed for the gig, and as he got close the woman swung round to eye the approaching rider, with apprehension showing in her face.

Doug pulled up about ten yards away and, raising his Stetson, smiled at her. The girl looked at him uncertainly for a moment as Doug appraised her dust-smudged face and jet-black hair all awry. Her long, black driving coat was equally dust-covered, but the answering smile that broke through, showing two rows of pearly teeth and two large shining, blue eyes, made him forget his own problems. He looked away to the gig, and the paint moving around stiffly to graze, and the large stone that had raised the right-hand wheel of the gig high enough to over-turn it.

'You all right, Ma'am?' Doug asked as he dropped to the ground.

'Yeah, I guess so now. I hit my shoulder when I fell out, but the pain wore off during the night.'

Doug looked at her sharply. 'This hasn't just happened then?'

She shook her head, and winced a little as a twinge of pain from her shoulder caught her. 'No, it happened after nightfall. It's my own stupid fault; I should have stayed in Chinooga Springs until this morning, like I intended.'

There was a quality about her voice that sparked Doug's memory; it was more mature than he remembered, but undoubtedly the same. 'You're Janet Huskisson, ain't thet so? An' before you tell me to mind my business, my moniker's Doug Machin.'

The girl stood stock still for a few moments, staring at him, before colour mounted on her face and she dropped her eyes. 'Of course you are, an' your sister's Sally, that right?'

'Well, I'm sure glad to see you again. Mind, you didn't treat me with much respect the last coupla times I visited with my pa. You were more of a tomboy than yore brother Sven.' He grinned to prove he bore no grudges, then became serious. 'How come you've been here all night an' no-one came lookin' for you?'

'Like I said, I should have stayed in Chinooga Springs. There's nobody in the Winged-O to come looking. I've been to see Ma and Pa onto the stage for Pueblo, an' Sven and the hands won't be back from Las Animas until tonight at the earliest.'

Doug nodded, then crossed to his pack-horse and collected an aparejo and one of the packs Sally had prepared, before returning to the girl's side. 'You'd better get yore-self outside that,' he said, 'an' after you've drunk yore fill, use the rest of the water to freshen yoreself up, while I get this gig back on two wheels.' Then, without further ado, he first crossed to the paint and inspected the animal, afterwards sizing the gig up for damages.

A couple of minutes later he crossed to where the girl sat on a small boulder, eating wolfishly. She masticated more slowly, when she found Doug's eye on her.

'I guess it's gonna be a coupla weeks before that paint's gonna fork anybody's weight or pull that gig,' he said, 'but that's no big deal. I can sling the gear my pack-horse is toting into the gig an' he'll give you no trouble. In 'bout ten minutes we'll have you rollin'.'

Doug was as good as his word. In no time he had the two cayuses roped to the gig, and putting his back against it he lifted and pushed as he shouted at them to pull. At the second attempt the gig came up and over, and the animals stopped at Doug's command. Tying the paint to the back of the gig, Doug fixed the gear onto his packhorse and fastened the animal between the shafts.

Janet Huskisson, now with the dust smudges removed from her face, watched the young rancher with interest, and marvelled at the difference between the callow youth of seven years ago and the man of today. She found him extremely attractive and, having admitted as much to herself, she perversely started to build up reserve. When she finally took her place and gathered up the reins, she sat prim and unsmiling, but Doug gave her a cheery smile as he climbed into the saddle and set off. Simultaneous with the reunion, so the location of the Winged-O came back to him. Not that he would have needed any pointers – the trail was plain enough; heavy wagons had worn ruts in places.

On the journey to the Winged-O, Doug rode for the most part close alongside the girl, admiring her lovely features, and warming to her as now and again she smiled involuntarily, despite her reserve, showing the pearl-white teeth between shapely lips, and big, blue eyes bright with humour.

They arrived at the compound in front of the ranch-house in due course, and suggesting to the girl that she went into the house while he saw to the cayuses, she agreed to leave him to it while she prepared a meal. Doug took plenty of time cleaning the trail dust from the three horses and fitting cold compresses to the paint's left cannon-bone, before binding it tightly with one of the long bandages he always carried. He gave them a drink and provided them with a good feed, before crossing from the stables to the house.

Janet Huskisson came to the dividing door to the kitchen upon hearing him enter, and pointed to a bottle and glasses on the table. 'Help yourself,' she said; then added: 'If you'd like to freshen up there's a pump out back, or you'll find a bowl an' jug of water with towels in the first bedroom upstairs.'

Doug nodded his thanks as he poured himself a drink, then after taking a mouthful said, 'I'll settle for the jug an' bowl, but I'll have to fork my freight pronto.'

The girl's face fell a little, then concern showed. 'I – I'm sorry; I didn't think. Helping me must have cost you a lot of time. Still, by the time you've freshened up I'll have a meal all ready, it won't hold you back any.'

'It smells good,' Doug said, before finishing his drink. 'I sure wish I had time to linger over it, but I've got a bounty-hunter on my tail, an' I'd like to keep plenty of space between us.'

'Bounty-hunter!' Janet echoed, her eyes rounded in surprise. 'What've you done to get a bounty-hunter on your trail?'

'I'm supposed to have killed Dave Caswall, the owner of the Flying Diamond, an' Sheriff Jake Caswall's whistled up Moss Hanney to bring me in.'

Janet registered horror, and she stared a long time at the young rancher. Then she shook her head in disbelief. 'I can't see you as a killer,' she said slowly. 'Not unless you had good reason.'

'I'm sure glad you think that way, Miss Janet,' Doug put in quickly. 'Back in Springfield it seems like folk don't have yore sort of belief. Mind, there's a US marshal an' deputy marshal working on getting me a fair trial just in case I'm innocent, but they're just not over keen on bounty-hunters on account they're too quick on the trigger. They like everyone, guilty or innocent, to get the full process of law.'

Janet gave a quick glance towards the cooking food before giving Doug her full attention. 'You go an' get cleaned up; you can answer my questions while we eat.' Then, as Doug made his way towards the stairs, 'Just how much lead have you got on that man Hanney?'

'Huh – enough I reckon,' Doug replied, with a smile. 'No need to get fussed. I led him a bit of a dance way back in the mountains.' With that he bounded up the stairs, leaving the girl to return to her cooking-range and attend to the sizzling viands.

When he returned a few minutes later Janet brought in two plates of mixed grill, then collected the coffee pot and jugs. Sitting opposite him she motioned him to get eating, and nothing loth, he attacked the meal with such evident enjoyment that she concluded he wasn't overmuch worried about the bounty-hunter, and most assuredly not guilty of murder. After more sober reflection she realized she was being foolish in presuming the latter. There were a lot of folk in these parts who could kill at the drop of a hat and were completely devoid of conscience. Watching him, and acknowledging that his good looks fascinated her, she found it difficult to believe he lacked conscience, but she decided not to delay him. The sooner he was on his way, the sooner she'd be safe, if indeed he was a killer.

Doug finished the meal with a sigh of contentment, and rolled himself a cigarette as the girl refilled his coffee-mug. She watched him light the cigarette and her heart seemed to twist in a spasm of pain as she pictured him in the bounty-hunter's sights, and despite her common-sense she found herself saying:

'There's no need to run any further. We've got a room under the roof where you could hide up, an' I could run those cayuses of yours up into the mountains.'

'No! – No!' Doug shook his head vehemently. 'There's no call fer you to do anything that'll put you in wrong with the law. I didn't kill Dave Caswall, so I'm not runnin' anywhere, nor hiding. At the moment I'm leadin' Hanney every which way, just spillin' out time until a coupla good lawmen get the right answers. Even if Hanney catches up I reckon my chances are as good as his.'

'All I wanted to do is give you time,' Janet Huskisson said, her face now tight drawn with concern. 'Sven an' the hands will be back later today an' they'd hold off that bounty-hunter until the marshals have finished their investigations.'

'No! I'm not gonna draw anybody else into my troubles.' Doug stood up as he spoke and came to within a couple of feet of the girl. He looked solemnly into her eyes, and taking her hand shook it gently. 'Thank you for the offer, Janet, an' thanks for the meal. I – I'll pay a visit when all this business is done, an' let you know all about it.' He half turned, then faced her again. 'Tell Sven what I've told you, an' tell him hello.'

She came to the door as he left, studying

his sturdy frame as he made his way to the stables, and she felt a need to be involved with him, to stand four-square with him. When, eventually, as he rode away, with the packhorse strung behind, he turned in the saddle to see her still framed in the doorway, and waved farewell, she was aware that the involvement she would like with Doug Machin went much further than standing side by side with him in his present troubles. Janet turned back inside the house full of concern for a man who, twenty-four hours earlier, although known to her, would never have crossed her mind.

Doug Machin, now heading for the quickest route to Las Animas, was trying to thrust the picture of Janet Huskisson firmly to the back of his mind, without a great deal of success. He knew he should be concentrating entirely upon his back, but rather than having qualms concerning Hanney, he was almost feeling beholden to the man for having set him on the run. If it hadn't been for Hanney he would not have re-met Janet Huskisson, and become aware of the transformation from tomboy to womanly beauty the years had wrought. He determined to remedy the omission of years and revisit the Winged-O at every opportunity, as soon as the question of his innocence became established.

Carl Travis had kept Hanney in view another long day, and now, just before daylight, he was ready once more to move onto the trail of the bounty-hunter, on what should be the last leg to Las Animas. Knowing he was downwind of Hanney, he rolled himself a smoke, and hiding the light from the tip with his Stetson, he enjoyed the sweet smoke he drew deeply into his lungs.

He had barely finished the cigarette before the sky lightened, and the deeper smudge moving away from where he knew Hanney to be camped told him the man was on his way, eager to be back in Las Animas. Quietly he climbed into the saddle, whispering to the big, shaggy-coated stallion, and he urged the animal to start the day. An hour later, with Hanney in his sight, he saw the man dismount and lead his mount behind a boulder, then Hanney lay full-length staring through a spy-glass down a long slope.

Dismounting, Travis moved to a better vantage point, and after trying half-a-dozen places he sighted at last what was claiming the bounty-hunter's attention. With difficulty he made out an overturned gig, two people and three horses. The distance was too great for recognition, but to the US marshal two people, a gig, and three horses, added up to Doug Machin and someone else.

He watched the gig being hauled back

onto its wheels and later a cayuse fastened into the shafts. One figure climbed into the gig and the other into the saddle, then they moved off to the west, the horseman riding alongside the gig. Travis turned his attention to Hanney, and the bounty-hunter was climbing into the saddle to head away to the left. Travis returned to where Red munched away at the long grass, and getting into the saddle he tried to take up a position where he could keep both Hanney and the gig in view.

Swinging Red around, he made for the lower ground and gave the stallion its head. As the animal hit top speed Carl got to wondering why Hanney hadn't immediately attempted to kill the rancher. He had been ready to take out Hanney if the man had made any threatening move, and it was certain that the bounty-hunter had been close enough to the figures alongside the gig to recognize Machin, if indeed it was the rancher. Even as he wondered, Carl remembered the stories he had heard about Hanney, and came to the conclusion that the other person had been a woman.

When he eventually came to high ground again, Travis slid out of the saddle just beneath the rim and crawled over the top to stare into the distance. He picked up the gig and rider first, then Hanney, patiently keeping the others in view, proving to Carl that the rider was Doug Machin. The marshal was about to slide back to his cayuse when he saw a section of a ranch-house further to the west, between rising ground and a thick windbreak. He checked the relevant distances between the ranch-house, the gig, Hanney and his location, and made his mind up quickly. He could get to the far side of the ranch-house, groundhitch Red and be in the house before the others would see him. Without hesitating, he regained Red's saddle and started his roundabout run to the ranch.

NINE

Moss Hanney picked up Doug Machin's trail by pure accident shortly after daybreak. Considering that both he and Machin were now lined onto the shortest route to Las Animas it was not surprising that their paths had now joined, but as neither was aware of the destination of the other Hanney could be excused a feeling of elation at the fresh sign that told him his quarry was almost within spitting distance. He drew back his black Morgan away from the trail and made for higher ground, always keeping the shoulder of the hill between him and the direction of the trail, and the first time he dismounted to check over the rim he struck gold.

Away in the distance he saw Machin's Stetson disappear over the brow of rising ground, and the packhorse quickly followed out of sight. Hanney permitted himself a tight smile. He knew exactly where he was, and all about the long slope that ran onto the trail between a ranch to the west and the Chinooga Springs to Las Animas stage route. He had ample time to make the cover of a massive boulder just over the rim, from where he'd make no mistake with his Winchester.

Gaining the shelter of the boulder the bounty-hunter took position and checked the Winchester, before returning his attention to Doug Machin, now in full sight. Then a sharp breath of surprise and pleasure escaped him as he took in the sight of the overturned gig, the grazing paint and the woman. In no time he had his spy-glass to his eye, and the appearance of the girl who was awaiting Machin's arrival with apprehension on her face had Hanney drooling with desire.

Luck was with him. What had become the most frustrating chore in his experience was now promising to be the most enjoyable. It didn't take him long to deduce that the gig had overturned the previous night, and the fact that nobody had come looking for her meant she was heading for an empty house. He made his mind up quickly to let Machin carry on his way, then take his pleasures with the girl before killing her and laying the blame at Machin's door. His lips drew back in an inhuman grin as he considered the girl, now talking to Machin, her face animated by a smile. 'I'll take thet smile off'n your face,' he thought pleasurably. He liked terror in his women victims to be the main emotion.

The Winged-O came into view, and Hanney was delighted to see that thick spread of trees forming the windbreak that overlooked the ranch-house and outbuildings. He eased

his mount away from the line he'd been following behind and south of the gig, and
when Machin and the girl had turned around
the far side of the cottonwoods, he crossed
the trail and made for the nearside of the
windbreak. By the time he had led the Morgan almost through the belt of trees, and
groundhitched the animal, Machin was leading the horses towards the stables and the girl
was passing through the door to the house.

Hanney celebrated by biting off a chew of
tobacco from a thick plug and settling down
to wait for Machin to take his leave. He was
in a fever of excitement thinking out his
intentions after the rancher had cleared the
ranch, and by the time Machin returned
from the stables to the ranch-house the
bounty-hunter had the added satisfaction of
knowing his surmise to be correct; there was
nobody else around the ranch. Once again
he thanked his luck; judging from the spruce
appearance of the ranch-house and outbuildings, the freshly creosoted corral rails,
gates and taut wire, there were precious few
days in a year when nobody moved around
the Winged-O.

Carl Travis studied the kitchen window, then
inserted the strong blade of his knife to push
the catch clear of its housing. It moved easily,
and a moment later he stood inside the
kitchen. Closing the window behind him he

moved quickly around from room to room. There were four bedrooms upstairs, and downstairs the kitchen led to the back from the large main room, and two smaller rooms led off the main room opposite the stairs. Carl reckoned the nearest to the side double doors was the ranch-owner's office, and the second one, furnished with delicate taste, to be the girl's retreat. He selected the latter as the place to lay up in wait for Hanney. With the door open just a crack, he would have a good view of practically all the main room. He checked his Colts and settled down to wait.

Within ten minutes he heard the gig and horseman arrive. There was a brief delay, then footsteps up to the verandah preceded a key being inserted in the lock and the front door was thrown open. A girl's footsteps crossed the big drawing-room and passed into the kitchen. The gig and horses moved off towards the stables. Twenty minutes passed by, with the smell of cooking tantalizing Travis, before he heard Machin enter the room. Later he heard the rancher stamp his way upstairs to get cleaned up, and later return and settle down to a meal.

He had heard Machin declare quite bluntly that he was being tailed by a bounty-hunter, and all the subsequent conversation between the two youngsters, and he was impressed by Doug's plain assertion that he was innocent anyway, and it was only a question of time before the fact would be established. That set him to wondering how Joe Wallace was progressing, and whether or not he'd been wise in leaving the young deputy to cope.

Dismissing the thought, he opened the door a little more and caught sight of the girl Doug referred to as Janet. 'Good enough to eat,' he thought. 'In the same class as the wives who waited for him and Joe Wallace back in Pierre.'

The girl brought in the coffee, and Travis drooled a bit as the smell merged with the sharp tang of tobacco as Doug lit up a cigarette. Then at least there was movement, and an exchange of words, before he heard Machin go down the verandah steps and head towards the stables. The girl remained at the door until Machin rode away and finally disappeared from view. He heard her deep sigh as she returned indoors to pour another mug of coffee.

Moss Hanney collected the thoughts he had allowed to fantasize during the past hour and a half, and willed himself back to the ice-cold calculating predator that was his norm. His lust-filled eyes were fastened upon the lissom form of the black-haired beauty who stood framed in the ranch-house doorway watching Machin's retreating back

139

as he walked towards the stables. He used his spy-glass the better to study her as she waited for the man to reappear, and he gloated in the knowledge that soon he would transform that calm exterior into wide-eyed, shaking terror as he stripped every vestige of clothing from her, before using her and killing her by the knife as she pleaded for mercy. A mad gleam came into his eyes as he laughed inwardly at the discomfiture of those US marshals when faced with Machin's guilt for such a crime.

Machin eventually led his two cayuses out of the stables, and climbing into the saddle set off to the north and was quickly lost to Hanney's view. The bounty-hunter's eyes returned to the girl, who stood in the door-way a further couple of minutes before stepping out on the verandah and waving a farewell to the departed rancher. When she moved back inside the house and closed the door the bounty-hunter sat back on his heels, content. He would wait a quarter of an hour to ensure that Machin was well out of earshot before he initiated the move that would bring screams of fear and despair from the woman inside the house.

With the time up, Moss Hanney eased his way through the edge of the trees to his left, away from direct line of the ranch-house windows, and slipped across the open space to the stables and outbuildings; then he sidled to the northern end of the verandah and cautiously climbed the steps. Stooping below the window-frame, he crawled under and stood upright at the door. He paused, savouring the surprise in store for his victim, then booted the door open with a thunderous crash.

Janet Huskisson gave a cry of alarm, dropped her mug of coffee, and sent her chair flying backwards as she stood up. The cry tailed off as she stared at the black-clad, macabre figure of Moss Hanney. With his piercing, black eyes set deep in his white, bony face, he looked what he was, the personification of evil, and together with a revulsion of horror the girl felt the horrible threat the man portended as surely as though he had spoken his intentions. With a struggle she found words.

'Who – who are you? What do you want?'

The smile that emanated from Hanney did nothing to reassure her. It merely heightened his devilish appearance. A gun appeared in his right hand like magic.

'Who I am won't matter a hill of beans to you when I'm gone, Ma'am,' he answered sibilantly. 'But so's you'll make it easy on yoreself I'll tell you. I want all you've got to give, an' I ain't talking 'bout dinero.'

As he spoke he came further into the room, and started edging around the table towards the girl, his eyes boring into her with hypnotic intensity, and Janet began to feel as powerless as the victim of a snake. Then with an almighty effort she pulled herself together.

'You must be tired of living, Mister,' she managed to say. 'My brother an' the hands will be here long before you get clear. They'll skin you alive if you lay yore hands on me.'

Hanney's lips spread further and he emitted a gurgle of pure delight before replying: 'Anything they'll find here will be the fault of the killer you just waved farewell to. When a woman entertains a killer she can expect to get molested an' mebbe killed. All I've gotta say is I just arrived too late. I reckon yore brother an' the hands will beat me to Machin an' string him up without askin' questions.'

'You're Hanney! The bounty-hunter?' Janet shouted, and she stepped back a bit further away, her eyes on a Remington rifle hanging on the wall. She edged towards it.

'Yeah – I'm Hanney, an' if you get any closer to the rifle I'll put a slug where it'll spoil yore enjoyment of what I'm gonna do next.'

As he spoke the last word he hurled himself upon her, and the man's tigerish strength took her by surprise. The gun he held hit her heavily in the back as he flung his right hand behind her, the blow sickening her and making her gasp with pain.

With the other hand he tore her jacket from her back and, grasping her skirt, ripped it away before hurling her to the ground.

Hanney's demoniacal laugh sent her blood curdling as he fell upon her; then she heard his sharp exclamation as his gun was kicked from his hand, and his body weight removed as she saw him thrown crashing onto the table and overside, to hit the ground over a chair; and a tall, angry-looking man stood staring after the half-stunned bounty-hunter. Janet struggled into a sitting position and noticed the door to her room was wide open. She pulled her skirt around her and watched the two men anxiously.

Moss Hanney extricated himself from the chair slowly, his mind clearing as he gained his feet. Instinctively, he knew now wasn't his best time to go for his gun, so he shook his head and let a bemused look spread over his face. He appeared to have difficulty focusing on Travis, but the lawman stood watching out of cold, dispassionate eyes.

At length the bounty-hunter allowed his eyes to show that he was now in control of himself. His mouth split in a sneering smile, and he nodded towards the girl. 'She needed the starch taken out of her,' he said. 'She's been harbourin' the killer, Machin. It's allus best to soften 'em up a bit; it saves 'em wastin' time with lies.'

'I heard it all, Hanney, every last word,'

Carl said quietly. 'An' you've reached the end of the road. I'm takin' you back to Springfield draped over yore cayuse.'

Hanney sneered. 'I thought you wus the hombre who stood out for fair trials. An' if you got me to a trial you couldn't prove more than I said. I wus only frightening the lady so's she'd tell the truth.'

'I'll give you to ten to go for thet gun, Hanney; then whether or no, I'm gonna put a slug into that hide of yores. Ten, nine, eight...'

Hanney shook his head as thought it bothered him, and he lifted his Stetson with a frown of concentration as Travis continued to intone. 'Seven, six, five, four, three...'

Carl Travis went for his gun as Hanney turned the crown of the Stetson towards him, and his Colt cleared leather and barked its message of death a split second before the Stetson went flying and the bounty-hunter staggered, stared wildly and disbelievingly, before clutching his breast and pitching onto the table, before slowly sliding backwards to the floor.

'You – you didn't count to ten,' Janet Huskisson murmured inconsequentially, and the marshal turned to look at her kindly, and shook his head.

'No. Just take a peek into that Stetson an' you'll know why. Now, why don't you get yoreself tidied up while I get this carrion outside, collect my cayuse an' Hanney's, then I'll tell you all about it.'

Janet's relief escaped in a long exhalation, and tears were very near as she tried to smile. Then she nodded thankfully and, averting her eyes from Hanney's corpse, hurried upstairs.

Travis dragged the bounty-hunter's body onto the verandah, then walked to the west windbreak and climbing astride Red rode back to the ranch-house, where he picked up the dead man's trail to gain the east wind-break via the circuitous route and ultimately pull up alongside the coal-black Morgan. He dropped to the ground and after tethering the Morgan to Red's cantle, eyed the leather saddle-bags the animal carried. He checked them as a matter of course, and in the second he found Hanney's telegraph from Sheriff Caswall offering him the chore of bringing Machin in dead or alive together with a wad of currency held together by red tape to the value of $500. He replaced both items in the saddle-bag, and climbing back into the saddle rode to the ranch-house where he tied the body over the Morgan's saddle.

Before re-entering the house he led Red into the stable, cleaned him down, fed and watered the animal, then brought a bucket of water and a nose-bag feed to the Morgan.

Janet Huskisson had cleared up and changed into a simple, severely-cut, black dress and was busily cooking something in the kitchen when Carl stepped back into the big, drawing room. He was carrying a towel, and with a word of excuse he walked past her and made his way out to the pump. As the girl kept an eye to the sizzling pan, and the coffee, almost at simmering point, she could not help now and again seeing the tall, handsome marshal, stripped to the waist washing away the trail dust, and admiring his muscular yet wiry torso. He seemed to exude quiet confidence.

When Travis returned the girl had a meal ready for him, and when he took a place at the table she brought in the coffee and poured two mugs before sitting opposite him. He smiled his thanks, then took a gulp at the scalding liquid before attacking the meal with real appreciation.

She watched him in complete silence until he had cleared every morsel and wiped the plate around with the last crust of bread. He pushed the plate away and drew the coffee mug closer, then he smiled at her, a smile that radiated his features, chasing away the stern serious air.

'Thank you, Ma'am,' he said. 'That was sure good.'

'Oh Marshal!' she exclaimed. 'You've no call to thank me. I'll everlastingly be in your debt.' Her beautiful eyes held him, her thanks shining out of them. 'I thought I was as good as dead. That man intended to submit me to every form to cruelty before killing me. I don't know where you came from or how, but to me it was a miracle.'

The marshal's face became serious again. 'No Ma'am, I guess it's my fault that things went so far that the last act was just in time. I was in there (pointing to the small room) before you an' Doug Machin arrived, an' I could've horned in at any time, but I had to let Hanney commit himself.'

The full impact of Carl's words sunk into Janet's brain, and her eyes widened in surprise. 'Why?' she asked.

He took time to build a cigarette, and got it lit before answering. 'I'm a US marshal, the moniker's Carl Travis incidentally, an' I'd heard rumours that Hanney always brought in the man he hunted, dead, an' in a lot of cases the hombres he was trailing committed the sort of crimes that he was just about to lay at Machin's door. I suspected that Hanney was the guilty one from the first day I saw him. I was trailing both him and Doug Machin, and from the moment Doug helped you with the overturned gig I guessed at what Hanney was intending for you. If he'd wanted he could have killed Machin there and then, but no, he was set on committing a crime which he'd blame onto Doug after killing him, an' Doug's trail would be there for all to see. That's why I rode ahead. I had to catch Hanney in a situation that proved what he was. All I can say is by sufferin' a little you've more'n likely saved a lot of folk from pain an' death by his hand.'

Janet nodded slowly, and a smile of understanding spread over her face. 'I'm glad you did things the way you did, Marshal Travis. The man was a monster, an' I'm glad he's dead.'

The smile was back on Carl's face as he stood up and pointed to the leather sofa alongside the wall. 'I heard you say that yore brother an' the hands will be back soon, an' in that case I'll get some shut-eye until they do. After yore trouble I reckon you'd rather not be on your lonesome just now.' When she agreed readily he crossed to the sofa, and when she looked across at him a couple of minutes later he was sleeping like a babe.

It was late afternoon when the thunder of hoofbeats brought Travis to his feet and caused him to join Janet Huskisson at the door to watch the Winged-O hands return. There were about fifteen of them ranged around a husky, handsome man in his early twenties who held some similarities of features to the girl. The riders stopped their noise and ranged their horses around the Morgan to study the corpse. Then they transferred their attention to Janet, and the lawman who stood alongside her. Barking an order to the hands, the owner dismounted and bounded up the steps while the hands moved their horses away, one of them leading the boss's Criollo towards the stables.

'Marshal Travis,' Janet said quickly, then, 'My brother, Sven.'

The two men eyed each other, then Sven turned and pointed to the horse carrying the cadaver. 'What's all this about?' he asked.

Janet led him inside the house and pushed him into a seat at the table, and she motioned Carl to a seat before turning back to her brother. 'Now why don't you get yourselves a drink while I hot up the coffee, then we'll tell you all about what's happened.'

Sven got up without a word, and fetched a bottle and glasses and poured two stiff measures before sitting back down and passing the makings over to Travis. He built himself a cigarette afterwards, and both men smoked in silence while they waited for Janet to bring the coffee. Travis marvelled at the other man's forbearance in refraining from asking any questions until his sister was ensconced in her seat. Then she told him all, quietly, in chronological order, and totally devoid of histrionics. She showed that she was now completely recovered from her ordeal.

Huskisson nodded slowly, his glance passing from his sister to the marshal, then he smiled and thrust out his hand to shake Carl's warmly. 'I'm much obliged to you,

Marshal Travis. There's no way me an' the hands can repay you enough. Anything you want, anytime, you just call on the Winged-O.'

Travis smiled and stood up. 'There's one thing that'd help me. Perhaps you wouldn't mind riding to Las Animas to let Machin know Hanney's no longer on his trail. Tell him he can get back to the Lazy Y as soon as he liked, an' me an' my pard will be in touch when we've prodded around some more.'

'Do I take it you're not going to hold him on the charge of murder then?' Janet Huskisson asked quietly.

The serious look was back on Carl's face. 'Doug was the last known hombre to have seen Dave Caswall that morning; but like I said, we've gotta dig around still.' He cheered up a little. 'Mebbe my deputy's turned something up since I left.'

'I sure hope so,' Sven Huskisson said fervently. 'I wouldn't have thought Doug Machin'd grow up into a killer, 'cept from an even start mebbe. Anyways, I'll be leavin' fer Las Animas just as soon as I've had some chow.'

'Yeah, me too,' Janet said firmly.

They accompanied Travis to the stable while he saddled up Red, and back to the house where he tied the Morgan to Red's cantle; then they stood and watched until he passed out of view around the windbreak.

TEN

Joe Wallace drew his bay mustang to a halt, and leaving the animal ground-hitched, eased his length to the rim of the fold to watch the Lazy Y gathering their mavericks out of the brush. Already a large herd of cattle grazed contentedly a few miles away, with only a few hands circling them, and much nearer a horse-wrangler looked after a cavvy of about thirty broncs. And in the middle of the valley two men worked with irons from a fire, branding the cattle that were driven near to the fire and brought down by the riders who had flushed them out of the brush.

One after another they came charging out, heads lowered and menacing, but the experienced Lazy Y punchers, waving their Stetsons, kept changing the direction of the mavericks' charge until they were close enough to the fire; then, roping the animals, and using the strength and skill of their cowponies, brought them down, and one of the two men with the irons scorched the Lazy Y into their hides, and the mavericks bawled angrily so that their noise reached the lawman.

Joe stood up and climbed back into the saddle, then headed downhill to the valley. He felt he should pose a few questions to Hank Ormond, and now was as good a time as any.

He made a detour to dodge the thick belt of brush and, hitting the valley between the grazing herd and the cavvy, he headed towards the fire and the bawling cows. He was getting close when a rogue steer blundered out of the thorns and cast a malevolent look around before charging at breakneck speed towards him. Two punchers followed close behind, and whilst the one started yelling and waving his Stetson to sheer the animal away, the other gave Joe a quick look then yelled and waved as he raced alongside the steer to keep it going on its course.

Joe recognized Hank Ormond in that brief moment before he was forced to act. He was left with nowhere to go, but managed to slew his mustang's head and shoulders to the right while his left hand streaked for his gun, and firing from the hip the bullet went straight into the maverick's forehead. The massive hulk almost touched him as it went into a stumbling faltering stagger, to crumble in an inert mass about twenty yards away. Hank Ormond hauled his bronc to a stop and glared at the marshal out of angry eyes.

'You gotta keep your eyes skinned, Marshal!' he exclaimed. 'Bein' raised in cattle country you oughta know you can't depend on a maverick bein' afeared of man nor beast straight outa the brush.'

As Ormond spoke the other rider turned away and rode off towards another steer just breaking out of the brush. Joe Wallace gave Ormond a cold look.

'I guess that maverick had no other way to go, the way you were yellin' an' wavin' that hat of your'n,' Joe said drily. 'That other hombre was set to guide it towards the fire, an' you know durned well you should have bin ridin' around him to help him.'

'What're you trying to say, Marshal?' Ormond snapped.

'Now ain't the time to dicker, Ormond. I've just got a couple of questions to ask you.' He paused while Ormond allowed his temper to simmer, then asked bluntly: 'How far did you keep company with Doug Machin on the morning Dave Caswall was killed? An' what reason did you have fer ridin' that morning?'

There was a guarded look in Ormond's eyes as he looked at Wallace sharply. Then he slewed in the saddle and pointed west-sou'west. 'See those two peaks – that's where the Lazy Y an' Flying Diamond part company. The Lazy Y's graze runs the west side of the east peak an' for 'bout twenty miles west of it. That east mountain is called Chinooga Peak, an' the Flying Diamond graze includes the whole durned mountain an' 'bout thirty miles south, an' twenty miles east of it. Wa'al, that's where I left Doug Machin the mornin' Dave Caswall got hisself killed. I needed to check a coupla lineshacks west of Chinooga Peak.' He paused, then added, 'Mebbe you know the west mountain is called Little Chinooga.'

Joe Wallace stared at the two peaks for a long time, while Hank Ormond watched him from under his almost closed eyelids. Both men ignored the mavericks being headed off towards the fire by dust-covered sweating punchers, then the marshal transferred his attention back to the ramrod. 'So for the sake of keepin' yore boss company you gave yoreself a heck of a longer ride than you needed to reach those lineshacks. You could've saved yoreself the trouble by headin' cross-country from the ranch-house, direct south-west around the Little Chinooga where the lineshacks lay.'

'Huh! The way I do my job is my business,' Ormond snorted. 'When I ride the LazyY range I guess I've allus got more than one reason. I like to check every inch of it, an' that was a good time to give the valley between those peaks the once over.'

Joe nodded affably, then snapped: 'An' what did you find at the lineshacks?'

Ormond shrugged, but took a little time in answering. 'The usual – provisions not havin' lasted out like they oughta, an' things not as tidy as I'd like. By the time we shove the beef we're not takin' on the drive onto that stretch of graze the lineshacks will be back to their proper state.' Seeing his replies appeared to satisfy Wallace, Ormond couldn't help pushing things. 'To my way of thinking, Marshal, you'd do better helping that pard of yores make sure Doug keeps a whole skin than riding around askin' folk fool questions like you've just asked me.'

Joe answered briefly. 'You've got no cause to worry 'bout Machin, an' if he didn't kill Dave Caswall he's not gonna get hung.' He made a move to ride away, but paused to give the ramrod a straight look. 'But the killer will!'

'Glad to hear it,' the ramrod said out of stiff lips.

'Something else you might like to hear,' Joe persisted. 'There's still a killer loose on this range, an' to me that points to some other hombre bein' guilty of Dave Caswall's killing, considering Doug Machin's bin under Marshal Travis' eye since he lit out.'

There was a momentary hint of pleasure in Ormond's eyes as he posed his question. 'Why? Who's bin killed?'

Joe took a long time in answering. 'Some buzzard shot Luke Withers from ambush at Henshaw Pass. I trailed that hombre all the way to the Lazy Y corrals.' Without waiting

155

for any reaction from Ormond, Joe set his mustang in motion.

As Joe headed away to the north Ormond stared after him, and he had to fight down a strong urge to put a bullet into the man's back. Before he pulled his bandanna back over his mouth and nose, he gave a thoughtful glance at the dead maverick and remembered the speed of Joe Wallace's draw and the deadly precision of his aim, and despite the extreme heat, a spasm of shivers ran through his frame.

It was late that night when the deputy marshal arrived back in Springfield. As he attended to his mustang after having let himself into the livery, Luke Withers came through the back door from the paddocks. They exchanged greetings; then, as the marshal brushed and combed the animal assiduously, Luke filled the manger with hay and a liberal supply of corn, and filled up the water-trough.

At length the marshal stepped back to admire his work, then made a fuss of the muscular mustang before leaving the stall. He grinned at Luke. 'I reckon you know where I'm headin' next?' he said.

'Yeah, my money's on the eating-house,' Luke replied with a smile. 'I guess I could manage to spin out the time with a coffee pot alongside of me, so I'll come with you.'

While waiting for Joe's meal to be cooked

they drank coffee and the marshal told Luke about his conversation with Hank Ormond and his narrow escape when Ormond had driven the steer at him. The livery-man stared at Joe in surprise.

'And you reckon that was a deliberate attempt to run you down?' Luke asked.

'Nothin' more sure,' Joe stated. 'I checked on the lineshacks, too, an' I reckon Ormond lied about them, unless he's had 'em provisioned since. They were all stocked up. Mebbe you can pay Miss Sally a visit an' find out if he's drawn stocks since the day Dave Caswall was killed.'

Luke Withers' eyes caught Joe's grin and he smiled in return. 'Sure thing. I'll be glad to set out first thing in the morning, just as soon as young Seth turns up. An' I'll be keeping a good lookout for bushwhackers, that's for sure.'

'I don't expect you to run into any problems this time, Luke. I sorta left the impression that the hombre who bushwhacked you the other day was plumb on target.' Joe's attention wavered as a Chinaman Luke called Ho San brought his meal to the table, but before he got busy with the eating irons he leaned across the ask Luke in lowered tones: 'Tell me, Luke. Is the sheriff still ridin' before sun-up?'

'Can't say fer sure, Joe, but I reckon so. He rode north this mornin' 'bout an hour before sun-up. If he was goin' in any other direction he'd have no call to pass close to the livery.'

Joe Wallace nodded, but it looked as though he'd lost interest in the answer. He was fully absorbed in his favourite occupation. Luke rolled himself a smoke and finished off his coffee before telling Joe he'd go and get some shut-eye so's to be up bright and early.

The next morning it needed three hours to daybreak when Deputy Marshal Wallace sunk into the shelter of the archway to the compound of Mallin's store, just a short distance from the stabling behind the gaol-house. The moon had already set and the stars, although bright in the sky, failed to penetrate the deep black of night, and the wind, as usual stronger at this time of night, searched with icy fingers through Joe's clothing, but he seemed impervious as he leaned against the wooden wall, waiting patiently.

His patience was duly rewarded. He had been waiting an hour when he heard the back door of the gaol open and close, before Jake Caswall's heavy footsteps crossed to the stabling. A glimmer of light showed through the space between the half-doors as Caswall lit a lamp, and Joe heard the jingle as the saddle was slung over an animal's back, then shortly afterwards the light went out, and Jake Caswall led his cayuse outside. The man grunted as he hauled himself into the saddle, then he moved off towards the south trail, and Joe noticed the peculiarity of gait that Luke Withers had mentioned, the sheriff's cayuse stepped light on his right foreleg.

When the hoofbeats died away Joe emerged from his shelter and tried the back door of the gaol-house. As he had expected, it was locked, so he took from his inside pocket a bunch of four standard-sized keys without a great deal of hope. He expected to have to spring a window catch-lock with his knife to gain access, but the third key did the trick, and the latch slipped back into its seating with well-oiled ease.

Once inside, the marshal pulled the blinds down over the windows. Then, with a lighted lamp in his hand, made his way around each room. The two living rooms upstairs he searched thoroughly, but found nothing of an incriminating nature, but in the bedroom his eyes lit upon a belt containing two Colt .45's and the doubts crowded in. 'Maybe Caswall had done the killing after all, and had toted the Navy Colt .36's purposely for years with the ultimate intention of providing himself with an alibi.'

Eagerly he extracted the guns, then one at a time he cocked the trigger and squinted at the lamp through the barrel. With a snort of disgust he replaced them in their holsters; both barrels were thick with cobwebs. He made his way downstairs, and apart from the two big drawers in the table either side of the sheriff's seat there was no place to hide anything.

It took Joe about five minutes to spring the catch on the drawers with his big hunting-knife, but about half-an-hour to sift through a miscellaneous collection of rubbish that had accumulated during the reign of half-a-dozen sheriffs. He was about to close the remaining drawer when the huge pile of 'dodgers' took his eye. They were held together with a large spring peg, and the thickness of the pile at the peg end seemed bigger than the loose end warranted, so he pulled them out and released the peg.

A satisfied smile appeared on Joe's homely face. He pulled a sheaf of 'dodgers' away to reveal one neat pile of dollar notes fastened with red tape to the value of $500 and another, which showed signs of having been rolled to fit a pocket, to the value of $350. A length of red tape lay in the drawer. Joe leaned back and allowed the thoughts running through his mind to settle into some sort of order, then being aware that the room reeked with stale tobacco he permitted himself the luxury of a cigarette. When he pressed the stub out in the already overflowing tin lid that served as an ashtray a plan had crystallized in his mind, and he liked it so much he couldn't restrain a delighted guffaw.

Tearing two bits of paper from his notebook he wrote his official rank and name on them and tucked one in the $500 wad of notes and the other he placed between the last and last but one 'dodger'. Then, fastening them all back in place with the peg, he returned them to the drawer and made his exit.

ELEVEN

Sally Machin ran to the window as she heard Luke Withers' gig roll to a stop outside the ranch-house. As she watched him favour the game leg in climbing down to the ground she felt a great tenderness for him, then as he looked up and saw her at the window his ready smile radiated his handsome features and Sally knew for sure that her feelings for him went far beyond charitable tenderness and concern, and with the knowledge making her heart beat like a triphammer she hurried outside to meet him.

Luke made to tie the Appaloosa to the hitchrail, but Sally took the reins. 'You go inside and fix yourself a drink, and I'll get this beauty unhitched and set him a feed. That'll make you stay a bit longer I guess.'

'I reckon you're enough reason for me to stay, Sally,' Luke replied, then he turned quickly to climb the steps, surprised at his own temerity, while the girl led the Appaloosa away, her eyes shining.

Soon afterwards the two of them sat facing each other across a table on the verandah, the coffee-pot between them, and Luke trying to build a smoke without taking his eyes

163

off the girl. She noticed his clumsy efforts and smiled inwardly. It seemed that she was having the same effect on Luke as he was having on her. Then in the midst of her pleasure the over-riding worry came back to her. She felt she had no right to any feeling of pleasure when Doug was still in danger from Hanney. Her thoughts became mirrored in her face, and her seriousness brought Luke back to the reason for his visit.

'There's something Joe Wallace asked me to find out for him,' he said, bringing the girl out of reverie. 'You remember the lineshacks that Hank Ormond was due to check when he left with Doug the day Dave Caswall was killed?' And when the girl nodded, 'He told Marshal Wallace that he found 'em, like always, short of victuals and dirty, so the marshal wants to know if Ormond ordered up provisions and had 'em sent out to the lineshacks?'

Sally Machin stared at Luke before standing up and going inside the house, and through to the storeroom at the back. She was back a few minutes later carrying a ledger. She turned to a page headed lineshacks and pointed to the last entries. Luke leaned over and saw the entries were dated eight weeks previously. 'That's the last time they were stocked up,' she said, 'but that's not to say it's all there now, and if Hank found them untidy it suggests that some hombres passing through helped themselves and laid up in them for a few days. It happens sometimes.'

Luke Withers shook his head. 'Nope, not this time. Marshal Wallace checked on them yesterday an' they were victualled up an' tidy. So it seems Ormond didn't visit the lineshacks like he was supposed to that morning. He hasn't done so since neither, or he'd have known they were all right.'

Sally Machin's eyes were sharp as she looked up. 'If he wasn't checking the lineshacks then, where was he?'

'I guess he could've been anywhere,' Luke replied, his eyes now on a small dust cloud to the south. 'But it's not up to us to find out. I'll pass on what you told me to Joe Wallace. I reckon he's got good reasons for asking.'

The dust cloud was bigger and soon a rider emerged from it, heading at speed for the ranch-house. Even at the distance Luke recognized Hank Ormond. 'Talk of the devil,' he muttered, 'here comes Ormond.'

Sally Machin slewed in her seat and satisfied herself with a glance at the approaching horseman, then looked back at Luke and leaned towards him. 'Luke!' she exclaimed. 'If he looks like staying I want you to take me to Springfield with you.'

Luke's surprise showed clearly, but he nodded readily enough. 'Yeah, I'll be glad to.' He stood up suddenly: 'Let's go back into the house; I want to see the way he looks when he comes in.'

Sally stood up without question and gathered up the drinks to follow Luke into the house, closing the door behind her. They sat at the far end of the table facing the door.

Hank Ormond pulled up in front of the verandah, and dropping to the ground tied his cayuse to the hitchrail. He wiped the dust from his face with his bandanna and took a quick look around at the bunkhouse and outbuildings before climbing the steps, and crossing to the door, opened it and stalked through. He stopped abruptly as he saw the couple sitting close together in front of him, and his jaw dropped at the sight of Luke Withers. He recovered quickly, but there was a bitter look on his face when he spoke.

'I thought you'd been salivated!' he exclaimed. 'That's what the deputy marshal told me yesterday.' He took a deep breath, then continued: 'I'm sure glad he told me wrong.'

Luke laughed. 'I reckon there's nobody more glad than me. It was no more'n a scratch. If I hadn't turned to look at a rattler I'd be dead now, the hombre was sure as heck on target.' He felt his head ruefully through the pad and bandage. 'What beats me is why any hombre wants to salivate me.'

'Mebbe your stablin' rates are too high,' Ormond said, with an effort to compose himself to normal conversation. He had spent the previous day with the belief in his mind that Withers was no longer a threat to him, and with Doug out of the way, now was the time to put pressure on Sally Machin. He'd intended to stay the whole day and night, even to compromise her if he could, and now, finding Withers alive and well, he determined to hang on after the livery-man departed and rush his fences. He started in by showing concern for the girl. 'I – I got to thinkin' if there wus a killer loose on the range, then you couldn't be left on yore lonesome here.' His look was full of concern as he directed his remark at Sally. 'So I decided to leave the hands knowing just what they've gotta do, an' stay here to look out for you.'

As he spoke he pulled up a chair and sat down. Luke Withers pushed the bottle and a glass towards him. The ramrod was in the act of pouring himself a drink when Sally replied.

'There's no call for you to stay, so you'd best get back to collecting the herd. I'm leaving for Springfield with Luke until Doug gets back.'

Hank Ormond spilled some of the liquor as her words drilled into his brain, and his eyes when he looked up at Luke were diamond bright and just as hard. He tossed the drink down his throat and struggled to regain his poise. 'Yeah,' he breathed at last. 'That's sure'nough good sense. I'll ride along when you leave an' have myself a few beers in town afore gettin' back to the Little Chinooga.'

Sally Machin stood up. 'I'll go an' pack a few things, then rustle up a meal before we move out. It'll be good to have you along, Hank, to keep an eye out for us.'

Somewhat mollified, Ormond nodded and stood up. 'I'll go an' see to my cayuse.' Then he turned abruptly and went outside.

It was about five hours later, and nearing Springfield when the gig with Hank Ormond alongside turned around the face of the canyon wall and they saw ahead of them the straight back of Marshal Travis astride the big, shaggy-coated stallion leading the Morgan bearing its grim burden.

Travis turned in the saddle, and seeing them drew to a stop. There were questions in the eyes of Luke Withers and Sally Machin as they got close, but Hank Ormond was filled with hate and bitterness. He had pinned his hopes on Hanney, and now it looked like Doug Machin was still alive. It struck him forcibly that if Travis considered Machin even a suspect for the murder of Dave Caswall, he would have brought him in to stand trial, and even if Hanney had killed his quarry Machin's body would have been brought in by the lawman. When he came to a halt alongside the lawman he felt the first tremor of fear. Travis and his deputy, Wallace, were dedicated and undeviating in their efforts to uncover the truth, and he searched in his mind for anything that might highlight his danger. But he could think of nothing, and when he greeted the lawman he had a smile on his face.

'Howdy, Marshal,' he said. 'Looks like Hanney bit off more'n he could chew at last.'

Carl slid out of the saddle, and as he walked back to the gig he merely said to Ormond: 'Yeah, Hanney got what he's deserved for a long time.' Leaning over the gig he shook hands with Luke Withers and addressed himself to the girl. 'Doug's all right, he'd gone on to Las Animas an' right now his friends Sven and Janet Huskisson have gone to Las Animas to tell him Hanney's dead, an' it's safe for him to get back to the Lazy Y.'

There were tears in Sally Machin's eyes as she leaned over to grasp Carl's hand. 'Oh, thank you, Marshal Travis, thank you.' Then, turning to Withers, 'You'll take me back tomorrow, Luke, so's I can be there when he comes home.' Luke Withers nodded happily, while Carl Travis shrugged her thanks away.

Carl turned to return to his cayuse when another thought struck him. 'I guess it's possible you'll have another guest to be ready for,' he said, with a smile. 'I can't see Miss

Janet losing sight of him yet awhile; it's my guess she'll be ridin' along.' Leaving Sally to tell Luke all she knew of the Huskissons, Travis climbed astride Red and forced the pace to Springfield. Ormond rode between the marshal and the gig, his mind a seething mass of indecision.

Arriving at the livery Carl waited for the gig to arrive. Ormond passed by, heading for the town, and as Sally and Luke stepped down Seth Paget came outside. He took in the scene and eyed Travis with respect before greeting Luke. Before they could enter into any conversation the marshal spoke to Luke: 'Can I leave you to get this hombre into cover an' stable my cayuse? I want to have words with Marshal Wallace before taking Hanney's corpse to the gaol-house.'

'Sure thing, Marshal. Leave it all to Seth an' me.' He grinned and added: 'If Joe's spending time thinking, you'll more than likely find him in the eatin'-house. It seems to help him.'

Travis smiled. 'Huh! So you've noticed. I'll look there first.' He tipped his Stetson to Sally, and giving Seth a friendly grin stepped off towards Main Street.

He drew a blank at the eating-house, but at the Panhandle hotel he pushed into Joe's room to find his protégé sitting beside the bed with sheaves of notes spread around the bed. Joe looked up and his eyes lit up with pleasure. He stood up and shook Travis' extended hand. Carl clapped the youngster's shoulder and nodded towards the notes on the bed. 'You got all the answers there, Joe?'

Joe nodded. 'I reckon I have. But how 'bout Machin. Where is he now?'

'On the way back to the Lazy Y from Las Animas,' Travis replied, 'an' Hanney's draped over his cayuse in the livery waiting fer me to collect and hand over to Caswall. Let's go an' get some chow and see what we've got between us.'

Joe Wallace agreed readily enough, and as soon as Travis had cleared himself of the trail dust, they made their way to the eating-house.

From the saloon section Hank Ormond stared at them as they crossed the road, out of hate-filled eyes. His taste for the drink palled, and he snatched up his Stetson, pushed his way out to the street, and un-hitching his cayuse, sprang into the saddle to ride out of town to the south, back to the herd at Little Chinooga.

They took a table well away from the few other diners, and while they drank coffee to spin out the time for their meals to be cooked, they got down to cases. Travis out-lined all that had happened since he took on the chore of wet-nursing Doug Machin in a matter of fact manner; the only time he al-lowed his feelings to show was when he recounted Hanney's perfidy. He shook his head in sorrow when he said: 'Makes me wonder how many good men died at his hand with a reputation for evil they didn't deserve.'

Joe itemised the investigations he had instigated and his findings, his lugubrious expression belying the depth of thought he had given to the case, and Carl listened with growing pride in his young deputy. When Joe went on to give his opinion of what had happened that morning when Dave Caswall was gunned down, and his plan for trapping the killer and bringing retribution onto the head of the man who knowing the killer, had used the whole situation to suit his own ends, Travis' smile of delight was the seal of approbation that told Joe he had passed his big test.

'One thing, Joe,' Carl said, as he built himself a cigarette. 'There's $500 in Hanney's saddle-bag, still tied with red tape, half payment for the chore of bringing in Machin I guess. We'll leave Hanney's corpse for Sheriff Caswall to handle, an' just give him an hour or so with the effects. You handle things the way you want.'

Joe took the makings his boss passed over, and gave his attention to the cigarette he was fashioning, hiding the big grin of pleasure and infectious good humour. Lin San came up with piled plates on a tray and from that moment until second portions had disappeared down his overworked gullet, Joe forgot about the case.

With the meal finished, they smoked another cigarette apiece and drank their coffee to the dregs, then set off to the livery. Seth Paget came up to them the moment they entered. 'You gonna take the cadaver now, Marshal Travis?' he asked, and when Carl nodded, 'D'you want your own cayuse?'

'Not now, Seth, but have both cayuses ready for us one hour from now.'

'Sure thing,' the youngster replied, and went out back to where he had Hanney's mount in the shelter of a lean-to, and unhitching the animal led it back to where the marshals stood waiting. Seth gave Travis a straight look. 'I reckon that hombre wasn't in the same class as the horseflesh he forked,' he said. 'That Morgan deserved better company.'

Carl, remembering the youngster's love of horses, considered Seth Paget gravely. 'I'm inclined to agree,' he replied. 'That animal deserves a hombre like you. If there's nobody with a claim to Hanney's effects, I'll see you get him.' As he spoke Travis took the lead rein and led the horse outside. Joe Wallace came alongside him and Seth Paget stared after them with something like hero worship staring out of his eyes.

The moment they hit Main Street the

crowd started to gather, and the shouted conversations rose to a crescendo of noise. A thousand questions were yelled at the two lawmen as saloons, dance-halls, gambling houses and stores emptied of humanity, and men crowded the sidewalks, and gathered behind the led horse to study Hanney's corpse. Hanney had never encouraged close contact in life and the way the front runners in the viewing stakes rapidly changed places, folk were no more keen for contact with him in death.

Jake Caswall became aware of the rising hubbub and with a curse he pushed his bottle away and staggered to the door. He thrust it open and stood outside to stare down the street. One glance was enough. The two lawmen, the coal-black Morgan and the black-coated figure draped over the saddle told the full story. He dodged back indoors and, holding the bottle by the neck, poured liquid courage down his throat.

Travis tied the Morgan to the hitchrail, then, unfastening the saddle-bags, carried them inside the gaol-house, Joe Wallace hot on his heels. Jake Caswall stared at them owlishly, but the cold, hostile looks of the lawmen chased away the alcoholic fog from his mind. Travis slung the saddle-bags on the table and pulled out the chairs for himself and Joe. Jake Caswall sank slowly in his chair, his eyes on the saddle-bags.

'You're a lucky hombre, Caswall,' Carl Travis said slowly. 'Machin's still alive. If that carrion draped over the cayuse had killed him on yore sayso I'd've put a slug between yore eyes right now. I salivated Hanney an' my report will go in to my office in due course, so I've no call to tell you why. You just get that buzzard to the funeral parlour an' buried deep.'

The lawmen stood up and glared at Caswall, hostile dislike in their eyes, before walking out, slamming the door behind them. Questions were shouted at them, but they ignored everyone as they made for the Panhandle saloon and ordered beers.

Jake Caswall took another slug of bourbon, then pulled himself together and pulling open the door glared at the crowd from the sidewalk. He picked out one of his old cronies and yelled: 'Get that cadaver to the funeral parlour, Jason.' And the man nodded, then asked: 'Who salivated Hanney?'

'Marshal Travis!' he barked, then, stamping back inside, slammed the door shut and eyed the saddle-bags thoughtfully.

TWELVE

Jake Caswall had just got himself believing he was out of the wood now that Hanney was dead. The US marshals would now surely move on. All he had to do was let it be known that he did not believe any longer that Doug Machin had been in any way responsible for Dave Caswall's death, and things would soon die down. Then the door burst open and Travis and Wallace stalked in and sat down. He stared across at them, apprehension in his eyes. Travis reached for the saddle-bags and emptied the contents on the desk. The lawmen looked at the desk then back to each other.

'Where is it, Caswall?' Joe asked. 'The $500 you paid to Hanney.'

The sheriff pulled a drawer open, and reaching in pulled out the notes and placed them on the table. 'Like you said,' he snapped, 'that's what I paid Hanney, half before he set out, the other half when he'd done his job. Well he didn't do his job, an' it's mine again.'

'Yeah, I reckon it goes along with the $800 you've got stashed away in the middle of those "dodgers" in the other drawer,' Joe went on. 'Money you took the mornin' yore Pa was killed, outa the box from the safe.'

Caswall stood up abruptly, glaring out of hot eyes. 'You're plain loco, mister.'

Joe shook his head. 'No, Sheriff Caswall, I'm not loco. $2,000 was taken from that box, we proved that with yore three brothers. We can add up $1,500 in yore possession right now, 'cept for the money you spent on that blonde we saw you with. You were there that morning, Caswall, an' you forgot to put the key back in its place, an' it was in yore hand when you pretended to find it on the floor in front of yore brother Sam an' the two hands. Wa'al, you took $1,500 for sure, mebbe someone else took $500, some hombre you know – an' before you say anything you might as well understand that we know, an' it ain't Machin.'

Caswall's mouth opened and closed like a fish and his eyes were glazed.

'Yore plumb lucky, Caswall, that we check everything out before jumpin' to conclusions. Things looked like you bein' the killer, but you ain't, on account that you tote Navy Colts that fire .36 slugs. Yore pa was killed with .45's.' There was astonishment on the sheriff's face as Joe continued: 'Now you've got one chance, an' one chance only. You'll bring in the killer pronto or we'll ride out to the Flying Diamond an' tell yore brothers everything we know. I reckon they'll stake you out for the buzzards.'

The thought of facing Frank, Sam and Clem had Jake's face working with fear, but there was no mercy from Travis and Wallace. 'The hombre you want left town a coupla hours ago for the Little Chinooga where he's got the Lazy Y hands gathering in cattle for the drive,' Joe told him. 'You've got twenty-four hours to bring him in before we pay a visit to the Flying Diamond.' Joe's expression changed a little and some warmth spread across his face: 'You bring the hombre in, an' you get to stayin' on as sheriff an' get the credit. Mebbe you've had yore lesson.'

The two lawmen stood up, pushed their chairs under the table and made their way to the livery, leaving Jake Caswall stunned and shaken. He helped recovery with a glass of bourbon, then sat back to consider his position. It took him half-an-hour to come to terms with things. All he had to do was bring in Ormond dead or alive and he'd be in the clear. He had no doubt that Travis and Wallace would keep their word and say nothing of his part in the affair. He made up his mind and checked his guns, then went out back to the stables and, saddling up, headed out of town past the livery, then west for Chinooga Peak and the Little Chinooga.

Luke Withers had called in at the livery and was still there when Carl and Joe returned to await the sheriff's departure. They moved deep inside so that they couldn't be seen by any passing rider and talked quietly about generalities. Luke was still basking in the bubbling euphoria of Sally Machin's pleasure in the knowledge that Doug was on his way home, and his cup of happiness was brimming over, when the tell-tale gait of Sheriff Caswall's cayuse told them the sheriff was on his way to bring in the killer. Joe Wallace immediately imparted the news to the livery-man so that he could put Sally's mind completely at rest. Beyond telling her, the lawman bound his friend to secrecy. They gave Caswall a half-hour start, then Joe led the way towards the place he had used to overlook the Lazy Y punchers previously. They were stretched out looking over the rim long before the sheriff came in view.

Jake Caswall's mind was a seething mass of indecision. Should he admit to his brothers that he had stolen $1,500 and knew the killer of their father was not Doug Machin, so leaving the revenge in their capable hands, even though it might mean he'd have to fork his freight and forego any claim on the Flying Diamond? Or should he try his considerable skill with his six-guns against Ormond, who boasted many known notches on his guns, and walk tall after the marshals

180

had left? Or should he lie up somewhere and put a slug in the Lazy Y ramrod from a safe distance, and take a chance on that satisfying Travis and Wallace? In the end he decided to give Ormond no chance. That way he could still walk tall.

Having made up his mind, he dismounted and transferred the derringer he had kept from the gambler, Shields', effects to his jacket pocket. At first sight of Ormond he could palm it, keeping it covered easily. When he got back into the saddle his confidence was fully restored and his prospects of the continued good life in Springfield seemed once again rosy. He even bit off a chew from a plug of tobacco and enjoyed the acrid taste.

His confidence remained with him right until he came out of a canyon beyond which the undulating plain seemed to end at the heights of Chinooga Peak and the Little Chinooga. Between him and those mountains was Hank Ormond, and his spirits dropped. He reached for the derringer and clutched it for comfort in a hand hot with perspiration.

All too soon Sheriff Caswall came upon the large herd of collected cattle, for the most part docile and chewing the cud, lulled by punchers singing their age-old ballads as they rode the edges of the herd slowly. The couple of riders who recognized Caswall gave him no greeting. The Lazy Y held no brief for him. He was the hombre who had laid out money for Hanney to bring young Doug in dead or alive. The sheriff felt their antipathy as he passed close to Norbett Long. The man looked straight at him, and with lips curling with dislike turned away. It helped to increase the tension and perspiration poured out of Caswall in streams as he rode away from the herd.

He passed the branding fire wide out, so wide in fact he could not recognize the two men sitting near the fire. Their job was nearly done, with brush steers now few and far between. The sheriff was now toying with the thought of keeping going, shaking the dust of Springfield from his feet. He had a $1,300 stake and he reckoned he could make Mexico ahead of Travis and Wallace. Then he was brought back to reality with a jolt; he might escape the lawmen, but he'd never escape his brothers. They wouldn't be bothered with the jurisdiction of the law once they knew of his part in things. They'd follow him to eternity. It was almost with a feeling of relief that he sighted Hank Ormond emerge from the brush behind two punchers who were directing a nasty-looking bull towards the fire. He tried to pull himself together.

Hank Ormond saw Sheriff Caswall the moment he cleared the brush, and instinctively knew the man's errand. Hanney was dead, the lawmen were allowing Doug Machin to go back to the Lazy Y, and Caswall had drawn his own conclusions or maybe had been forced back to act on what to him was knowledge. Anyway Ormond knew what he had to do.

The two men closed the distance and came to a stop ten yards away from each other. Ormond looked at Caswall from under slitted lids.

'Wa'al? What in heck do you want? It must be something mighty special to get you off'n that butt of your'n.'

'I've come to take you in, Ormond, for killin' my pa, Dave Caswall,' Caswall found himself saying, and the perspiration poured from him anew.

Ormond made no attempt to deny the charge, and his voice held a sneer. 'Only one way you'll do that, hombre, so you'd better reach for 'em.' He saw the fumbling movement of Caswall's right hand and Ormond's hands flashed to his six-guns.

Jake Caswall's hand, wet and slippery with perspiration, failed to get the derringer into position, and in the last despairing moment of his life it slipped from his hand to the ground. Ormond watched the sheriff slide out of the saddle with a contemptuous smile on his face.

Dropping to the ground, Hank Ormond

183

ran his hands through the sheriff's pockets, and his spirits rose to a high level when he transferred the bundles of currency to his own pockets. Then, climbing back into the saddle, he rode directly to the chuck wagon. To Curly Waters, the cook, he merely said as he dragged out his saddle-roll: 'Jake Caswall got a bit uppity. I'll take him into town. Just tell the hands to call it a day an' get those beeves onto home graze.'

Curly Waters merely nodded, but he noticed when Ormond had fastened his saddle-roll and regained his seat in the saddle, that the ramrod headed south.

Carl Travis and Joe Wallace looked at each other after the drama had been played out within their vision, and grim smiles showed on their lips. 'I guess that's the way we thought it'd go,' Joe said. 'Let's see how Ormond will play it from here.'

Travis' smile broke into a grin. He liked the way Joe was progressing. He nodded, and said: 'The wind's in our favour; let's have ourselves a smoke.' As they built themselves cigarettes they watched Ormond go through Caswall's pockets and transfer something to his own before riding away to the chuck-wagon. What he did there was beyond their vision, but shortly afterwards they saw him ride south.

Joe Wallace took a long look south, then

back at the rider's trail direction and the position of the sun. 'He's gonna ride around the west side of Chinooga Peak, an' I guess I've just go 'nough time to nail him before sundown.'

Carl Travis held out his hand and shook the youngster's firmly. 'He's fast Joe,' he said, 'but he's not in yore class. I'll tote Caswall into town an' look in at the Flying Diamond to tell his brothers he died trying to bring the killer in. I reckon those hombres needn't know anything bad about their brother.'

'You're durned right,' Joe replied. Then he was gone, sliding down to where his big, bay mustang cropped contentedly, and springing into the saddle rode around the Little Chinooga. Travis picked his route down to the valley to where a few Lazy Y hands stood admiring the corpse.

Joe kept to the folds and gullies, hiding himself from Ormond's view, in his race to where a narrow valley separated the Little Chinooga from Chinooga Peak. Across that valley and just a couple of miles on, Chinooga Peak rose in a stark, almost vertical wall, and the foot of the mountain was cluttered with boulders the size of cathedrals. He stopped his mustang where a fold nearly gave out on the breast of the mountain, and took a quick look over the rim. He was well ahead of Ormond, and if the ramrod continued in the same direction he reckoned he would be able to cross the valley and wait in hiding close to the trail that carried on to Des Moines. Then, back in the saddle, he concentrated every nerve and sinew on his chore, and the big mustang stuck to its task with all the power and grit it possessed. So with Ormond unsuspecting, Joe waited behind a massive boulder for the ramrod to appear.

No more than half-an-hour was involved, but to the waiting marshal it seemed an age, and the shadows were lengthening with the dying sun. Then at last he heard the un-hurried hoofbeats, and judging things just right Joe rode his mustang onto the trail. Ormond was just fifteen yards away.

Surprise showed briefly on the ramrod's face, then he looked calmly at the marshal out of hooded eyes. 'You come to help me look fer strays, Marshal?' he asked with a grim smile.

'Nope. I've come to head you off from wherever you're goin' an' take you in fer the murder of Dave Caswall an' the attempted murder of Luke Withers,' Joe replied calmly. 'I guess you just killed Jake Caswall from a standin' start.'

Ormond took a deep breath. He had nothing to gain by denial, the young pup of a marshal knew it all, so the marshal had to die. The ramrod had complete confidence in his ability to outdraw any other hombre, so he allowed a sneer to show on his lips. 'If you're gonna take me in, Marshal, you're gonna have to be quick enough with those irons.' As he spoke his hands blurred for his guns.

They were clear of leather and levelling when the two slugs thudded into his heart, and Deputy Marshal Wallace watched him express surprise before pitching out of the saddle.

It was the work of ten minutes for Joe to tie Ormond's remains across the dead man's saddle and to start the journey back to Springfield with his chore done. Joe reached for the makings and allowed himself the smoke as a celebration for the successful conclusion of his first case.

Early the following morning the news had reached the Lazy Y, and Luke Withers pointed out the best way to reward Joe Wallace, at least, and had offered to make for town in the gig to talk to the US marshals. When he returned to the Lazy Y it was with the firm commitment on their part to look in later, and he brought with him young Seth Paget, leaving his father to look after the livery.

When Carl and Joe were halfway to the Lazy Y, the hands passed them en route for town and celebrations and they all stopped to shake hands cordially with the lawmen before continuing their jubilant way. Coming to the ranch-house, they saw the cattle on home graze ready for the drive, and Seth Paget rushed down the steps to take their broncs to the stables, telling them to go inside.

The two men stepped inside the door and stared wide-eyed at the table that practically groaned under a spread to beat all others, and they were pulled inside, Joe by Sally Machin and Carl by Janet Huskisson.

It was a long night, yet it went in a flash– Good fellowship treats time that way. But in that time Doug and Sally Machin, Sven and Janet Huskisson, Luke Withers and Seth Paget all thanked the lawmen for their own and several reasons – the youngster, Seth, for Travis remembering to tell Luke that Hanney's Morgan was to go to him – and both men were pressed to promise they would always look in at both the Machin and Huskisson spreads when passing any-where near, and the livery.

Before they left, it was obvious to them that Luke Withers would be marrying Sally Machin, which augured well considering Doug's regard for Luke, and Janet Huskisson seemed determined not to let any more years slip past without sight of Doug. So when Seth Paget brought their mounts to the front, and the whole crowd waved and cheered them off, Joe turned to his boss with a grin.

'We've still got a coupla days left. How about lyin' in bed late an' feedin' our faces an' generally spoilin' ourselves?'

'You shouldn't let one case go to yore head,' Carl replied. 'But yeah, mebbe you've earned it.'

The publishers hope that this book has given you enjoyable reading. Large Print Books are especially designed to be as easy to see and hold as possible. If you wish a complete list of our books please ask at your local library or write directly to:

The Golden West Large Print Books
Magna House, Long Preston,
Skipton, North Yorkshire.
BD23 4ND

This Large Print Book, for people
who cannot read normal print,
is published under the auspices of

THE ULVERSCROFT FOUNDATION